MARTHA

MARTHA
Trinity of the Chosen

C.S. EVANS

To Keith
Best Wishes

C S Evans

BREWIN BOOKS

First published by
Brewin Books Ltd, 56 Alcester Road,
Studley, Warwickshire B80 7LG in 2016
www.brewinbooks.com

ISBN: 978-1-85858-551-2

A Cataloguing in Publication Record
for this title is available from the British Library.

Typeset in Haarlemmer.
Printed in Great Britain by
4edge Ltd.

I dedicate this story to
all those in search
of a *truth*...

ACKNOWLEDGEMENTS

So many have helped me along the journey of MARTHA. They have held my hand and encouraged me with words of wisdom and knowledge. Special thanks go to the people of Wales, who are guardians of such beautiful soil. The owners, staff and visitors of the 'Owl and The Pussy Cat' Tearooms and Restaurant in Laugharne, where I would sit pondering the next chapter. All those at 'Portreeve Restaurant' who allowed me to quiz them whilst keeping me well fed. My home town, Birmingham, for its abundance of wildlife and creatures that need protecting. Catherine Brown (aka Charlie Brown), Lorraine Swoboda, Mike Davies and my publishers Brewin Books who all had faith in my story. Finally, a heartfelt thanks to Suzy Gallier, who had the patience of a saint when it came to keeping me on track.

CHAPTER 1

Now was my time, all 1800 seconds and it fed my appetite for routine. My eyes fixed on a small patch of ceiling where the paint had missed the white. Normally, my obsessional behaviour would start eating away at me and I would curse the fact that my Mother had been sloppy with her work. It was 5 o'clock, my most precious time of the day. The last year had thrown my life into chaos and despair, changing it forever.

I knew it was only a short time before my Father would be home, but I excelled in precision and accuracy. Every minute that passed followed a methodical pattern; the ceiling was always the first to be inspected. However this evening was different; I felt calm and at one with my bedroom: I could forgive this tiny imperfection as I was going away. Gazing at the curtains, I followed the pleats that fell neatly down to the soft lilac carpet. Each of the four walls kept my thoughts secret and never questioned why the face that belonged to me was the way it was, lacking in emotion. I would never allow a picture or mirror to distract from their simple beauty or reflect my plainness.

Everything in my room was lilac, from the hand-painted wardrobe that my Mother had lovingly stripped, to the nail varnish on my chest of drawers. I never wore it, but it reminded me that one day I may grow up to be a normal woman. There was no television, mainly because after much searching, one could not be found in the right colour. I also had no time for staring at a screen where people were false and laughed from a script, as my life had become a script. Checking the room to make sure everything was in its place, I gave a sigh of relief. I looked at the time on my phone; it was 17:05. Normally, at this precise minute, I would take off my school uniform and hang it up neatly for the following day, my shoes always put in the same box under the bed, but today I would keep them on for a little longer. My school books would not be put in alphabetical order on the shelf above the bed, but remain in my bag.

It was the 23rd July and the last day of term, my final GCSE had been completed and I no longer had to suffer the enduring company of others. All of my teachers had shown surprise that I'd even been capable of attending school at all these past twelve months. I had been offered endless counselling sessions by my Form Tutor.

"If you need to talk to someone then I can arrange it. It is not healthy to keep things bottled up inside you."

"No thank you" I would say politely, why would I want some stranger, who probably had no experience of life themselves, unpicking my thoughts; they would also expect me to cry and bottling things up was my way of life. She would have wanted me to carry on studying, it was important to her that I concentrated on things that made me happy; after all I was going into Art and Design at Edinburgh University and I had made a promise. I would continue with my studies, ignoring all others around me, then take flight to a walled city, leaving behind memories that nightmares are made of. I might even develop a Scottish accent and no-one would recognise my voice.

Father was due home at 17:30 and the familiar sound of the key in the door would prompt me to shout downstairs, "Shall I put the kettle on?" And his reply would always be the same, "not too strong, Matty, and no sugar, I'm sweet enough."

The mobile she'd brought me, said it was 17:10, so I had another twenty minutes to ensure the room was perfect. There was one thing that wasn't lilac; a silver photo frame sat proudly on my chest of drawers. I'd asked her to paint it, but, after a long discussion about how silver couldn't be painted and how it was a family heirloom, I had relented. She knew all about these things, her job had taken her all over the country and across the world. Her ability to turn the most uninteresting characterless room into something magical made her one of the most sought-after interior designers. Everyone recognised her work by the lilac stamp she left behind. Somehow she would sneak it into the wallpaper or carpet; furniture would shine and chandeliers would catch the colour, casting it out in fragments of light across the room. All looked well for me in my space, nothing to move, giving me time to close my eyes and plan our summer break. My Father had been allowed to take all his annual leave at once and so we could escape from everything that had happened.

I had scheduled everything; the first stop would be Edinburgh: I wanted to know more about the city before I moved there. Famous for its burial sites, I was hoping I could finally bury something myself. The next stop would be the Lake District, as I desperately wanted to experiment with water colours; perhaps they would bleed across the paper, my pencil lines and brush strokes no longer having a rigidity. After that, Oxford, to breathe in the library and to smell the must of printed paper, maybe even find the lost book. Finally, we would head down South and end up in St Ives: the sea breeze would put its arms around me, giving me comfort and taking away my bad dreams. However my list meant nothing, hours of planning had upset him and I didn't want this. He had enough distress to fill an ocean full of tears. He wanted to break all my rules and go on a journey where time and place didn't matter, and wherever we ended up would be a release for him, so I gave in.

Brighton was first on his list. When I was younger, my Mother would tell me about the splendours of Brighton Pavilion and its cosmopolitan town. The lush colours of the Pavilion and over-the-top gilding enthralled her, I knew she longed to take her favourite colour and paint over some priceless antique. Thankfully she never did, the shame of being arrested and violating some crazy old Prince's furniture would have meant the end of her career, but she had fun talking about the possibilities.

After Brighton, he decided we would just set off and see where the car took us, but we had both agreed there was one place we would not go. I longed to hear him laugh for the first time in nearly a year, desperately seeking places where no one would know us. "It's for the best, Martha," he said.

My mind had gone ahead of itself and I hadn't checked the photo on the dressing table. I got up from my bed and walked over to where it always stood. It was taken on their wedding day and my Mother's smile filled the frame. She was more than beautiful; her curly auburn hair fell over her shoulders and rested on the delicate lilac lace of her wedding dress. Her green eyes were gazing up at my Father and his hands were gently resting on her tiny waist. Around her neck lay a fine silver chain from which hung a small silver fox. He towered above her like a giant, 6ft 4 inches tall and hair as black as ravens' wings. Now he was grey, almost white, but shock can do that; I'd read it in a magazine, but my Father said it was nonsense.

"Matty, I know biology isn't your best of subjects, but you should realise it's all down to genetics." I was constantly checking my hair for a sign of a silver thread.

They'd met at Birmingham University; he was in his final year studying Law and she was in the last year of her Fine Art degree; two completely different people, one carefree, the other methodical, both connected by love. She'd moved from Wales, leaving behind her endless beaches that hadn't enabled her to fulfil her ambition. After leaving university, he'd gone to work for Fellows & Martin, a well-established law firm based in the city centre, and it paid well. My Mother found it more difficult to find a job and ended up as a curator at Birmingham Art Gallery. She had no love for the stuffiness of the place and would recount tales of mischief and the longing to daub her favourite colour over the walls. "Thank God you didn't," my Father would say, shaking his head with disapproval, "The Pre-Raphaelite collection would never be the same." He loved the wild and crazy side of her, but always breathed a sigh of relief when she was being sensible and level-headed.

After six years she became pregnant and eventually decided to go it alone and set up her own business; she longed for the freedom of being creative and became an interior designer. It also meant she could work from home and, when I was old enough to start school, she was around to take and collect me. My friends at school found her amusing; she would turn up at the school gates in ball gowns with feathers in her hair. On one occasion, I came down with chickenpox and she collected me wearing a 1950's lilac dress and matching tiara: I say friends, but I had only one true friend.

My phone rang. I should have remembered to put it on silent and the stillness of the room came to an abrupt end. Why hadn't I remembered to switch it off? I cursed myself. Everyone knew not to call me between 17:00 and 17:30, so it must be someone who'd dug through bins and found my number. I'd lost count of the times my number had been changed. If it was the press, their number usually came up unknown and then I wouldn't answer. I grabbed the phone off my bed and looked, it was Lizzie and all sense of fear left me, quickly replaced by irritation.

"What's up, you must know the time?"

"Oh come on Martha, for God's sake, can't you just loosen up a bit. I thought that for once a few minutes earlier wouldn't make any difference."

"Well, it does, I've got loads to do and Dad will be home soon."

Lizzie knew me better than anyone and tolerated me more than most. She had been there for me, understanding my condition. I forgave her, I always did, even when she would deliberately move something round in my bedroom and time how long it took me to find it. I had got it down to five seconds and told her she was slacking.

"How did the maths go, do you think you nailed it?" she said.

"Not sure, think I did OK, but you never know." There was a long pause and I could imagine Lizzie grinning with anticipation, waiting for me to ask how she'd done.

"So, how was it for you? I bet you struggled to get past the first question." She knew I was teasing more than jealous.

"Mine was a breeze, I tried to make the final question last, otherwise I'd have just sat there bored silly."

This came as no surprise as Lizzie was incredibly bright, she was a walking calculator. We'd known each other since junior school and everyone looked up to her. Everything seemed to come so easy to Liz and nothing bothered her. When it came to secondary school, I felt as if my life had fallen apart. Her parents had chosen a different path for her, one that they felt was more educationally challenging; they had great plans for her and I was sure she would fulfil them. She'd probably end up being a top consultant in Harley Street, marrying a heart surgeon, having a daughter called Harriet and breeding Great Danes. She was everything I wanted to be, small with hair the colour of corn and freckles that covered every inch of her face. Time didn't matter to her and she could laugh until she cried.

"You around tomorrow? I was wondering if you wanted to go into town?" she asked.

"I have to pack, Liz, but you can come here, you can help me pack what I have listed and double check that I haven't forgotten anything."

"You mean you haven't already done it? It's not like you, Matty. Have you and your Dad decided where you're going?"

"Brighton's first on the list, then I'm not sure where we are going next."

There was a short pause before she gleefully said, "Well, Martha, there's some hope for you yet." I could hear her giggling, she knew me so well. I'd tried to persuade my Father to plan the whole summer holiday, but he wanted none of it.

"How exciting, Matty, you may end up in Paris or Rome."

My heart felt as if it was skipping a beat at the thought of leaving the country, filling me with dread: What if the police called? What if someone knew something? She may come back.

"We can chat tomorrow, Liz, I'd best get off the phone as dad will be here any minute, shall I see you in the morning about ten?"

"Ok, Martha, say hi to your Dad for me and tell him my folks are up for a drink one night, it's been ages since they've been out together."

"Will do, I'm sure dad would like that when we get back from holiday. I'll ask him when he gets in and let you know tomorrow, see you in the morning."

I hung up the phone and noted the time, it was 17:27. In three minutes I could smooth out my bed sheets from where I had been sitting and ensure all was as it should be. 17:30 came and I went on to the landing and waited. Any time now I would hear the familiar sound of his key turn in the door and the thump of his briefcase on the hall tiles. A newspaper would be placed on the table and his coat slung over the carved mahogany stand. I was hoping that tonight we could order a takeaway and I could show him the list I had made for us. My phone was the first thing and a priority to me. It kept perfect time and watches always gave me a rash, so I never bothered, and, besides they could go wrong. What seemed like an age passed and there was no sound of my Father. I looked at my phone again, it was 17:36. Taking a deep breath in, I tried to convince myself there must be a good reason. He was never late, even though his job demanded so much of his time; he would always continue working in his study after supper. He knew he needed to be back for me, he understood my ways.

It was 6 o'clock when I heard the key turn, sweat had collected in the nape of my neck and my hands were shaking. The key sounded different, somehow hesitant and awkward, as if it didn't want to go in the lock. The front door opened slowly and he walked into the hall holding his briefcase, which appeared to be weighing him down more than normal. There was no newspaper under his arm and he turned to walk into his study keeping his coat on.

"You're late! How come you never sent me a text?" I snapped.

He looked up at me, his face looked drawn and his eyes darker than normal.

"Sorry, Martha, I had to stay over for a while and had a meeting with Mr. Fellows, I'm going into the study for an hour, we can talk about supper later."

Later, I thought, what the hell's going on? What about his usual cup of tea? He never went into his study this early. I was furious, how dare he, he knew how much routine means to me. I ran down the stairs, nearly slipping on the last two steps, grabbing the bannister to stop myself falling. The study door was closed. I knocked and waited, but there was silence, apart from the sound of my heart beating. Normally, I would never dare to enter his study if the door was shut, it usually meant he was up to his neck in paperwork or on the phone to some hysterical woman about her divorce. This was different and I'd not seen that look on his face since the summer of last year; he must have heard something, I thought. I turned the handle of the study door and strode in, determined to confront him about his behaviour. He was sitting on the old leather sofa and paperwork was strewn around him. The pink ribbon that usually bound it all lay on the floor. "Oh if only they would let you use lilac," she would say. Time and time again, he would explain the history of the ribbon, originating from the 17th Century when all legal documents were tied with red cloth. Over the years it had faded to pink and it was the tradition for all lawyers to use it. "Hence the red tape rubbish," he would say with his deep laugh, and "No, you can't change it!"

In his hand he held his favourite glass, engraved with his initials, S.J. whisky had covered the letters, making them seem small and insignificant. He never drank on a Thursday, it was always on a Sunday after supper. The dishwasher would be loaded, he would shower and then say "Martha, pour us a little drop, only up to where the S starts." This always gave me a sense of importance, as my Mother would have done it for him in the past, making sure it never flowed past the engraving. He was staring into the glass, swishing it around, making the whisky splash over the sides, falling into golden droplets on the carpet. He raised it to his mouth and downed it in one, wiping his lips on the edge of his coat sleeve.

"What the hell's going on? Are you sick? Have they been in touch? Tell me now!"

He looked up at me and, for the first time since he came home, his mouth turned into a slight smile.

"No sweetheart, I'm not sick and I haven't heard anything, God knows I wish I had."

A wave of relief came over me, but then my frustration and anger began boiling back up inside me.

"So, if you're not ill and there's no news, then what's up? I had hoped we could order a takeaway tonight and go through the list I have made. Oh, and by the way, Liz's coming round in the morning to help me pack."

I did my best to appear relaxed and show him I was calm, after all we were finally going away. Remembering how my Mother had shown me how to attempt a smile, I moved my mouth as best I could, hoping this was convincing enough. I walked towards him and sat on the sofa; placing the documents and papers in a neat pile, picking up the ribbon off the floor, I bound them back together. People's lives were tied up in those papers, grief, money, jealousy, death and anything that required his knowledge of the law. The chaos in his study never seemed to bother him, but it bothered me. She always kept it tidy for him, singing around the room and dancing with her duster, "Dust, dust go away, plague the lawyer another day." I would get up early and give the room a good clean, Lizzie would help me. My Father reached over and held my hand, his eyes staring hard into mine. We were like mirror images of each other, there was no mistake that he was my Father. I was 5 ft 10 inches and still growing, and my eyes were as dark as his. When he frowned, I frowned; I was the daughter of Stuart James for sure.

"Matty, I need to tell you something."

He paused and before he had chance to carry on speaking I shouted out. "You have lied to me, you have heard something, I knew it!"

"I have always promised I would tell you if I had, but I haven't and we need to come to terms with the fact we may never, but I have to go away for two weeks. I'm so sorry, but our company's been taken over by an Australian firm of lawyers. They want me to go to Melbourne to meet the new directors." He paused. "If I don't go, then they will find someone else to take my place. I can't afford not to. Please try and understand Matty, it's only for a short while and I'll make it up to you. We can go on holiday afterwards."

"You can't go!" My words screamed and I let go of his hand, knocking the whisky glass from out of his grasp. The glass shattered on the floor leaving tiny fragments of his initials deep within the carpet. "You made a promise and Mr Fellows said that, after last year, you could take this break!" My hands were now clenched into fists and I pressed them down hard into the leather of the sofa.

"I know I did and I'm sorry, but I've already lost so much time off because of last year, the new company won't honour the agreement. You have to understand, Martha, it's out of my hands."

My brain whirred like a finely-oiled machine, this could be sorted and there must be an answer.

"Well I'll come with you, then. That's it."

"Matty, I've thought this through and looked at every possible solution." He looked down at the shattered glass avoiding my gaze.

"It's only for a short time and the two weeks will fly by, we can take off wherever we want then."

He looked up at me and his face seemed to soften. I knew the pain he had suffered over the past year and I wanted to put my arms around him, but I couldn't. I felt frozen to the spot and those sorts of emotions didn't come easy to me.

"Well, I'll ask Lizzie to stop here until you get back, there's a solution for everything." I got up from the sofa and walked towards the telephone on my Father's desk, treading on some broken glass, I felt a sharp piercing pain in my foot, but that pain I could deal with.

"Stop this now! You know that's not fair on her or her parents. What if the police find anything or the press start hounding you? You can't stay here, you need to be somewhere safe, Matty, with someone who understands."

Understands, I thought, how could anyone comprehend what we've been through, the endless sleepless nights waiting for any news. Men camped outside our house with cameras pointing in our faces like grotesque masks, wearing stained pinstriped suits and breath that smelt of stale tobacco. There were phone calls from people who offered help, but turned out to be sick individuals with nothing better to do.

"I"m sorry, Matty, but there is only one choice, you have to go back."

I knew immediately what he meant and I could feel every drop of blood drain from my body.

"You have to go back to Pendine."

CHAPTER 2

"I dream of foxes on sun-kissed soil
With golden eyes that rise at dawn
And when he walks towards my past
I'll bow and pray my dreams will last"

My Mother was staring out through the French windows, they were wide open letting the July sun stream through. I could see the sadness in her eyes as she gazed out at the garden, but she had good reason to feel this way. Her small delicate hands were resting on the door frame, slowly stroking the wood as if it was a living creature. She had done most of the painting throughout the whole house and was proud of each brush stroke. Her team of decorators was not allowed to step foot in her domain.

Turning towards me, she smiled, "Come and help me pick some roses for the dinner table."

Her outstretched hand grasped mine and she led me down the steps from the patio to where the rose beds lay. It was a hot and humid afternoon, the garden was alive and vibrant with colour. Red Admiral butterflies were resting on the buddleia bush and the air smelt sweet from thyme, mint and camomile. I could hear the sounds of the radio blaring from the kitchen and the smell of coffee permeated every room of the house. The washing machine was whirring and spinning all things lilac and wafts of fabric conditioner and soap powder were making a heady Sunday perfume. It was the day when we were all together, no distractions or phone calls about what colour carpets should be used or if my Father could save a betrayed wife from eviction. My homework had been completed and all my lists done, I'd showered and inspected every inch of my pale ghost-like body for blemishes, there was no room for imperfections on my skin.

After dinner, my parents would sit on the sofa, holding hands as if it was their last day on earth. Tomorrow, my Mother would be travelling back to Wales to see my Grandmother. The previous month, my Grandfather had died, leaving no will to his estate, and my Grandmother had demanded my Mother return home to help sort out all the finances.

"Meredith, why on earth don't you let me sort out this mess?" my Father said, "There's no need for you to go back, I can deal with it here."

She refused, "Stuart, you know damn well it's a conflict of interest and it will give her another excuse to despise you."

He knew this was true; my Grandmother hated my Father and blamed him for everything. In her eyes, my Mother should have gone back home to Wales after finishing her degree, after all she wasn't a city girl and Birmingham would be her downfall. In truth, my Grandmother just wanted another person to control and manipulate; she was a bitter and twisted woman.

We stood looking at the roses for a while, their crimson petals bathing in sunlight; it seemed cruel to cut them down in their prime.

"Tell me what Grandfather was really like?" I asked, knowing she would tell me the truth; my Mother never lied.

"What would you like to know, Matty? You know he loved you very much." Her eyes were still full of sadness, but it didn't cloud the emerald green that shone within them.

"I want to know more about when you were young, not when he became older and Grandma said no to everything; did he ever laugh Mom?"

"Of course he laughed, Matty, what a crazy question. Don't you remember the time he took you down to the beach and you went in search of crabs amongst the rocks where he slipped and fell in a large rock pool? When he climbed out he was covered head to toe in seaweed and you called him 'The Green Welsh Dragon'; he laughed that much that he slipped and fell back in again."

All the sadness suddenly left her eyes and her smile returned; the garden seemed even more colourful now. I never understood why he found my words so funny, I was just telling him the truth. He was green from the seaweed and his expression was one of a creature breathing fire; he was also Welsh, but he had joy in reminding me that Welsh Dragons were red. Why was this amusing, I wondered, but then I remembered that others around me laughed when I did not. I had been taken to the doctors to see if I could get any help. The doctor had told my Mother I could be on a spectrum.

"What sort of spectrum?" she asked.

I just sat there staring out of his surgery window wondering what colour on the spectrum I was.

"Well there's different types of spectrums, Mrs James, and Martha is bordering on one of those. It is difficult to diagnose at the moment."

"Well excuse me for being stupid," she retorted, "I would like to know what spectrum you're talking about."

He shook his head and said, "I wouldn't worry about it, she's healthy and bright and may just grow out of it. These sort of children are often blessed with a gift. We could send her off for tests, but I think it is too early on, come back and see me in a year's time."

That was the last time I saw a doctor about my so called 'spectrum' and I was left wondering what my '*gift*' was, and, each day following, I woke up expecting to find it. I used to imagine it would be under my pillow, wrapped up in paper.

"So why was he so different when Grandma was around?" I asked, passing my Mother the secateurs. She then cut the first rose and handed it to me.

"Your Grandfather never wanted to move from Tenby. He was a gifted jeweller who could make the finest things using Welsh gold and silver." As she spoke she put her hand up to her neck and stroked the silver fox that hung from its chain. "He should have stayed there, but your Grandmother wanted to move, running a bed and breakfast house was her idea of keeping an eye on him." She laughed out loud and cut another rose. This time a thorn caught her thumb and she jumped back, blood trickled down and tiny droplets fell onto her dress.

"You OK?" I asked, more concerned that her dress had a stain on it and it clashed against the colour.

"I'm fine, darling," she said, as she sucked her thumb until the bleeding stopped. "Would you like to see the new project I'm working on? I'm really excited about it, Matty."

She gazed down the garden to where her studio was. I suddenly felt confused, she never allowed me in there until she'd completed her client's work. I would occasionally be allowed to see photos she had taken after they had paid her bill and were satisfied.

"You sure Mom, they won't mind?"

"It's not up to them, and you may give me some more ideas of your own, start young I say." She placed the roses carefully on the grass and started to skip down the gravel path towards the studio.

"Come on, dinner's not ready yet and your Father's probably knee-deep in paperwork."

As I watched her go down the garden, she seemed to transform into a younger girl. Her bare feet made no noise and her auburn hair looked redder than normal.

How can people get younger as they get older? Why do I look so much older than I am?

I followed her down to the studio, it was brick built and the width of the garden. Either side of the door were two large windows that you could see straight into.

"Light is the most important thing when you create," she would say, "without light you cannot see shade and without shade you cannot see darkness."

As we entered, I was hit by a blaze of colour I'd not seen her use before. There were fabrics of burnt orange and gold strewn across her work table, like a lush carpet of golden hay. I looked around and there were sketches of boats and barges hanging on the walls. Bulrushes stood proud in glass jars and wild thistles were scattered over the floor. This was not like my Mother's work, it was as if some artist from a foreign land had wiped her canvas clean and painted a vivid landscape using the sun's rays. The old bookcase still stood proud along the one wall; it reached from floor to ceiling and she had brought it up from Wales when she moved.

"Worth a fortune, that is," she would say. "Take care of it for me, Matty, lots of hidden mysteries and beautiful words lie on those shelves."

"Where's the lilac?" I almost choked on the words. "There's nothing in here that hints at it, have you put stuff away?"

"There is none in this project, Martha, I'm designing the interior for a boathouse and it will be beautiful; lilac will be back, so don't you worry. I've moved all my paints and catalogues to my office in town, I needed the studio to be clear for this job."

A sense of unease came over me and I put my index finger on my wrist to check my pulse. My Mother laughed, she knew me well and was never irritated by my obsessional habits. Routine was my life and I needed to feel safe, my self-built cage was always around me, secure and locked – the key had yet to be found.

"Calm down Matty, it's still crazy little me, this is just a one-off experiment. The gentleman who owns the boathouse knows my usual style, but wanted something different. Sometimes we have to step outside of the box and take a risk, only once perhaps, but make it majestical." She walked towards her couch and sat down, patting her lap she said, "come, let me explain."

I sat down beside her and could smell the sweet perfume she wore, not too heavy, but delicate like a flower that had yet to be discovered. I rested my head in her lap as she stroked my hair. My straight black locks fell down towards my waist and she lifted each strand high up into the air, her fingers like the finest tooth comb.

"You are beautiful, you know, I don't think you realise it sometimes, I'm so proud of you, Matty."

Beautiful was not a word I would use about myself; I was tall for my age and none of my features were in anyway striking. My face was one that could be lost in a crowd and my mouth hurt if I tried to smile. I could smile if I concentrated hard, but soon found it slipping back to its normal position. I remember a friend at school once describing a famous actress as being '*ugly beautiful*', perhaps that was me. I was not unhappy, far from it. Happiness to me was safety and taking risks filled me with dread.

"Yes, that colour is my trademark and always will be, it has been with me since I was a young girl."

I looked up at her, puzzled and confused. She had never told me that before, but then again, I had never asked.

"Your Grandfather's death has made me think hard about life and the way I work. He was never allowed to take any risks, your Grandmother made sure of that. She controlled everything he did, from the time he woke up until the time he went to bed. Perhaps that's why I'm rebellious and not like your friends' mothers. However, Matty, there is part of me that likes safety and my favourite colour gives me that."

Now I was getting more confused, this was all new to me and I didn't like it.

"Routine is good for everyone, Martha, without it we can't function. It gives us a living and a good foundation for life. Sometimes taking a risk opens up a new chapter in our character; we should run like wild animals and let it take us to places we've never been." Her soft Welsh lilt seemed to make her words sing.

"But I can't do that, I'm frightened." I buried my head deeper into her lap.

"There's nothing to be frightened of, Matty. I would never let anyone harm you. Come on, tell me what you think of my next project."

She stood up and moved towards one of the drawings on the wall. She had sketched a large boathouse overlooking a river. Her pencil lines were soft and flowing and I envied her ability to do this. Drawing came easy to me and, from an early age, I could replicate buildings with great precision, but they never flowed like hers, this was not my gift. The boathouse was supported by tall wooden pillars which towered over the water. It had a large balcony and the timber frame looked tired and in need of paint; perhaps she would paint these lilac.

"Isn't it beautiful," she said, "the view from the balcony is breathtaking. I've started work on the inside, I'll show you some photos." She walked over to her office desk and pulled a handful of photos from a draw. "Let me know what you think," she said as she passed them to me.

As I looked at them, I felt as if I was being let into a world I'd never seen. Each room was as rich as the next, golden fabrics adorned the windows, paintings of wild animals in gilt frames hung on each wall. The living room had a large stone fireplace and my Mother had painted it a deep red. The whole room looked as if it was on fire, but one that wouldn't burn the skin.

"It's certainly different, it's not like anything you've ever done before. Where are the flowers and tree prints, aren't you leaving your trademark?" I questioned with wide eyes.

"I am leaving my mark, Martha, but this is one with a risk. I may have got it wrong, he may not like it, but this feels right." Her expression was one of delight and excitement and she looked more beautiful than ever.

"Have I always been serious?" I asked her. "People at school think I'm strange."

"Well now, let me think." She took the photos off me and sat back down on the couch; her smile comforted me a little.

"We are all unique, none of your friends are the same as each other. Wouldn't life be boring if we all wore the same expression on our faces? Some people's minds are different and they find it hard to relate to others. People find different things funny, and some are more thinkers than doers."

"So what am I, Mom? And you know I have only got one friend."

She paused for a while before answering, then finally said, "You are a mixture of all things, you think before you act. You like to ask lots of questions, and in answer to your first one, yes you have always been serious. This isn't a bad thing, Matty, and as you grow older you will change. People that you meet will make you smile and laugh, you may even meet a boy soon that makes you feel like you've never felt before."

"A boy!" I exclaimed. "I'm not interested in them. All the ones at school bore me to tears and they are so scruffy."

Now I was irritated and my mind drifted back to school. There was a boy in my class that had shown interest in me a few months back, but his hair was untidy, he smelt of cigarettes and he was always late for school.

"I'm not sure I want to change, things seem to get complicated if you do." Now it was my turn to try and smile. I put each index finger either side of my mouth and pulled.

My Mother laughed out loud, then put her arms around me tightly. "You be whatever you want to be and your Father and I will love you no matter what. My Father loved me for all my quirkiness, even when my Mother disapproved. It's a shame you didn't get chance to get to know him better." The sadness soon returned to her eyes. "I think he worked too hard to try and please my Mother, but missed being creative with his hands and having a free spirit. Your Grandmother has always been driven by money and that house was all she ever wanted. He would get up at 5am in the morning every day to start preparing breakfast for the guests, and it would be gone midnight before he went to bed. Even when he became ill and frail, he carried on making sure the house and garden resembled a small stately home, and I think his last days were spent worrying what would become of it."

I thought back to the rare occasions when I had visited them with my Mother, being told to be quiet in case the guests heard, tip-toeing along hallways and hiding behind closed doors. My Grandfather would take me down to the beaches, where we would fly a kite or watch the skies for planes that were on practice manoeuvres trying to break sound barriers; I would hold my hands up to my ears as they passed overhead waiting for that loud bang. He checked his watch constantly staring up towards the hill, never seeming at ease; perhaps I was like him.

"Am I like Grandpa, is that why she's never liked me?" Yet another question I thought, but always an honest one.

"You are a unique mixture of all of us, Martha, especially your Dad." She twirled my hair around her hand then lay it gently on my shoulder. "Talking of your Father, we'd better go and see what he's up to. I bet he hasn't checked on the dinner, I'm sure I heard the oven timer go off." She walked towards the door and beckoned me to follow her, "Time for food, the brain can't work on an empty stomach and I am starving."

As we walked back towards the house, I picked up the roses that lay on the grass. The heat had made them wilt slightly and, as I stroked the petals, my mind was taken back to my Grandparents' house. Perhaps water would bring them back to life, I thought, I couldn't help but feel we had left them out too long and they would die.

When we got back to the house, I could hear my Father whistling from the kitchen, the sound of pots and pans clattered and banged and it began to feel like a normal Sunday again.

"Where have you been?" he asked, his face flushed with steam from the cooker. "The chicken will start to resemble a budgie if it's not taken out soon." My Father was not a great cook. He'd tried many times to impress us with his culinary experiments, but the bin was always their final resting place. My Mother found it easier on all of our stomachs to cook, and neither of us complained.

During dinner, we talked about my Mother's journey back home. She had decided to catch the train to Tenby, then get a cab to her Mother's house.

"It's not often I get chance to take a train," she said. "I can work on my sketches and soak in the scenery."

She normally drove everywhere, filling her car with all her samples of materials and ideas for the next client, but she was adamant that this time she would relax and enjoy the journey. They spent the rest of the afternoon in the lounge together; I thought it best to leave them and, besides, my bedroom was calling for me. Sometimes I thought I could hear it whisper my name, but I never told anyone. People already thought me odd and strange enough, so explaining would be a waste of time. After my usual half hour, I decided to get my sketchbook out and attempt drawing the boathouse my Mother had so lovingly captured. I started with the pillars, but my lines were precise and looked rigid, so I tore the paper up and threw it in the bin. It was then I heard raised voices coming from downstairs, it sounded as if my Mother and Father were quarrelling, so I went on to the top stair and tried to listen. I'd never heard them row before, perhaps the odd dig or tease which had got out of control, but this sounded like a full-blown argument.

It was coming from the living room and my Mother sounded distressed. Father was shouting and I could hear her trying to answer him, but her sobs were stifling her words. Arguments never happened in our house, our perfect family stayed calm whatever life threw at us, and I'd never heard him raise his voice like this. Suddenly the living room door opened and I raced back into my bedroom. It wasn't long before there was a soft tap on my bedroom door and my Mother's face appeared.

She entered the room and I could see immediately that she'd been crying, no longer looking a young green-eyed girl, but a woman whose face looked tired and aged.

"What were you arguing about Mom?"

"We weren't, Matty, your Dad is just a bit stressed at the moment, don't let it spoil the rest of the evening. Why don't you come downstairs and we can all watch a film together, you can choose."

"What time are you off in the morning Mom? Is Dad taking you to the station?" I took a tissue from my pocket and handed it to her, her eyes were less red by now and she seemed a little calmer. A tear had dropped on to my carpet and left a stain; why had she lied to me?

"I'm off really early, so you sleep in angel; your Father's dropping me off on his way to work. I will call you later on in the day when I get to your Grandmother's. You know how lead-lined the place is, so I probably won't text. Getting a signal round there is a nightmare, I'll use her landline, and no doubt have to pay for the call!" She let out a laugh and her smile returned. "Come on, let's go downstairs and have a nice evening," with that she walked out of my room.

I would miss her, the woman I wanted to be, but couldn't and never would be. I followed her downstairs; my Father was waiting for us in the sitting room and the TV remote was in his hand.

"You pick, as long as it's not a zombie or vampire film," he said, looking at my Mother and grinning. "Your Mother will be meeting up with a vampire when she goes back to Wales."

The rest of the evening we spent together, my Mother joked about wearing lilac glittery trousers to meet the solicitor and my Father made notes and a list of questions that she could ask him. I decided I would spend the next three days trying to perfect my drawings and perhaps experiment with watercolours. If the paint ran and seeped across my structured lines, then this would be a way forward and perhaps there was hope for me.

I kissed them both goodnight and made her promise to call me as soon as she could. Sleep came easy and I dreamt of boats moored to a house that floated in the sky. It was alive with colours of orange and gold, and the boats were as grey as a night storm. In one of them was a small figure, it was waving to me frantically and I desperately tried to wave back, but my arms were too heavy.

That was the last time I saw her and the night my life changed forever.

CHAPTER 3

"Hello, police please." My Father's hands were trembling as he tried to keep the phone steady against his mouth. He hadn't shaved and grey stubble covered his chin, dark circles lay under his swollen eyes and the night's lack of sleep had taken its toll.

My face showed nothing; numbness and shock were there, but lying deep under my skin. I'd tried desperately to cry, and earlier, I'd splashed water on my face. Looking in the bathroom mirror, I thought it would help him to see me in distress, but there was no taste of salt. I was cursed like an expressionless manikin, a doll that could only blink when shook. As I watched him, waiting, I wished it had been me that had disappeared, no-one would notice if I had gone. It was mid afternoon, 15:22 to be precise, and the air was oppressive. Black clouds descended, and in the distance, I could hear the rumble of thunder; we were in for a storm in more ways than one.

"I want to report someone missing." There was silence in the room as he waited to be transferred to the police station.

I looked around, our living room was exactly the same as she'd left it. All was in its place, newspapers had been put in the rack, the cushions on the sofa had been plumped up and, in the dining room, a 'to do' list had been left on the table. There was nothing to indicate she wouldn't be back, no farewell letter or note saying goodbye.

It seemed an age before my Father spoke, his words stammering. "It's my wife, she was supposed to contact me last night and I've heard nothing." He paused and I moved closer, trying hard to listen to the person on the other end of the line.

"Yes, I've checked," he said. "Her Mother hasn't heard from her either, she was going back to Wales to her parents' house and was

22

due to meet a solicitor early this morning, but hasn't turned up for her appointment." His voice was now desperate. "Please, can you help me? It's not like her not to be in touch." There was silence again as he waited for a response. "Thank you, it's Fern House, Lickey Hill Road, we are the end house on the left. Can you tell me how long you'll be?"

I noticed the clock on the mantlepiece had stopped ticking, I went over to it and took the key, winding it up, making sure the time corresponded with my phone. It stood on a small marble base and now the ticking was the only sound that could be heard. I walked back to where he stood, counting each tick and it gave me comfort.

"Ok, I will." He put the phone down and turned towards me. "They want all contact details of who she was due to see, pass me a pen and paper, Martha."

I snatched an envelope and pen from the table and he started to scribble down names and numbers, his hands were still shaking and his writing was illegible.

"Here, let me do it, they won't be able to read a word of that."

I took the pen and paper and neatly numbered all the contacts in capitals, there was no excuse now for them to misread anything.

"She'll be back, I know she will." I said, desperately trying to sound convincing.

"The police said they will send someone round, but they couldn't give a time, can you think of anyone else she could have met up with, Matty?"

The only friend I knew she was close to in that area was her old school friend who lived in Laugharne. Perhaps she has met up with her and got waylaid.

"What about Sara? I think her number's on a post-it note on the fridge, I'll go and look."

Now there seemed a light at the end of the tunnel, that was it, she'd met up with Sara, maybe had too many glasses of wine and stayed over and lost track of time.

I ran out of the living room along the hallway into the kitchen. Light streamed in through every window and the black marble work tops sparkled and shone, stainless steel saucepans hung in order suspended from the ceiling, she'd cleaned the kitchen from top to bottom. On the front of the fridge door were the post-it notes, held down by fridge magnets from all over the world. She made a point of buying one from every place she worked in. There was a Welsh red dragon holding down a yellow post-it and I grabbed it and ran back to the living room.

"Here it is, give her a call," I said as I passed it to him. He quickly dialled the number and waited.

"Hi Sara, it's Stuart here, Meredith's husband. I'm wondering if you can give me a call when you get in, it's rather urgent." He placed the receiver back and stared out the window, the sound of thunder was getting nearer. "She must be at work and, hopefully, the police will be here soon; why don't you go and rest, Matty? We've both been up all night and you must be shattered."

This was true, neither of us had slept, we'd waited and waited for her to call and my Father had been ringing my Grandmother on and off for hours.

"I'm not going anywhere until they arrive, I want to know what the police can do. I'll wait here and you can make yourself look more presentable, you need a shave."

"A shave for Christ's sake! That's the last thing on my mind." His eyes flared at me, piercing like a knife.

He was upset, I thought; perhaps it was better he was left alone and I could go and check all the rooms again. After a couple of hours I had gone through every room in the house, I heard a car pull up the drive; it came to a slow steady stop and then the sound of two doors clanked in unison. Surely, if it was the police they would have a siren going, but then again to them there was no emergency. People go missing every day, the news was full of people appealing for their lost relatives. I was in the dining room, the 'to do list' was still on the table and the smell of polish hung in the air. Our house was easy to maintain, there were no nooks or crannies. On the inside, it was modern and cubic, but on the outside a mock Tudor front gave it the impression of a building from the past. She liked the quirkiness of it and said the builder must have been to see a Shakespeare play one night then watched a science-fiction movie the next. I looked at the list again and it showed nothing out of the ordinary, water the plants, put out the recycling bin and my Father was to post a parcel for her. The rest were just gentle reminders to switch things off at night and get supper in for her return. Return, I would show this to the police, it meant she intended to come back and I willed myself to think she was just stuck somewhere that had no phone signal, but she was safe.

My Father appeared. "Martha, the police are here and they want to speak to both of us."

I grabbed the list and followed him back to the living room. Two officers were stood in the doorway, one was a middle-aged man who looked far too overweight for his uniform, he was losing his hair and had tried to comb what little he had forward, the other was a young woman who looked not much older than myself. She was blonde and her bobbed hair sat neatly on her pressed collar. I thought she was far too pretty for a policewoman and much better suited to advertise lip gloss.

"Hi, you must be Matty, my name is PC Charlotte Drayton, you can call me Charlie if you want, and this is my colleague, PC David Mayer."

"I shan't call you Charlie." I said, "I don't know you well enough. Please call me Martha, only my parents and my friend call me Matty."

PC Mayer smiled, "Oh, we are sorry Martha. We would like to get some details from you and your Father regarding your Mother not being in contact."

"She hasn't just not been in contact, she's gone missing." I couldn't help myself, were they stupid as well as rude?

Surely you need qualifications to join the police force or were they desperate?

"Martha, we need to help these officers in anyway we can, come and sit down and try and be a bit more polite, I know you're upset, but they are here to help." I could see my Father was frustrated with me so I sat down and decided to hold my tongue.

"Mr. James, can we have your wife's full name and date of birth?" Charlotte produced a black note book and pen and waited for him to speak.

"Her name is Meredith James, 30th August 1971. Do you need her birth certificate, I can go and find it if it would help?"

"That won't be necessary Mr. James, at the moment we are just making a general enquiry, that will do fine." The policewoman started writing and said, "that's a pretty name, I've not heard of it before."

"It's Welsh," I chimed in, "most people pronounce it incorrectly, she gets furious if they give it that merry sound."

"Well then, Martha" said Mayer, "you tell us how it should be pronounced." The overweight officer took off his helmet and placed it on the coffee table.

"It's Meredith as in Mer-Rheh-dith, you can cheat and say M'redith if that makes it easier, as long as you say it right, she says it means *'protector of the sea'*, strange really as she can't swim."

"Strange," he said, "why strange?" He looked at me puzzled and I decided I didn't like him, I also wondered if he was married and why his wife hadn't put him on a diet.

"When was the last time you had any contact with your wife, Mr. James?" Charlotte asked.

"It was yesterday morning. I dropped her off at Birmingham New Street station on the way to work, she was catching the 08:42 train to Tenby, changing at Bristol Parkway and then Swansea. She was getting the local train to Tenby, then catching a taxi to Pendine."

It then struck me that my Mother's journey was far more complex than I'd realised; I'd assumed she was getting a direct train. She could have stopped off anywhere along the route, anything could have happened.

"What was the reason for her trip, Mr. James?" Mayer asked.

"She was going to visit her Mother, her Father has recently died and there is a lot of legalities to sort out. My wife was due to see her Father's solicitor early this morning. I've already spoken to him and he hasn't heard from her."

I held out the neatly written note I had made and offered it to Charlotte. "All his details are on here, and my Grandmother's contact number, you can call them if you want."

"Thank you Martha." She took it from me and placed it at the back of her notebook.

"Mr. James, how did your wife seem when she left, was she distressed in any way, or did she seem unwell?" Charlotte asked.

"She was fine!" My Father had started to become agitated and was pacing up and down the living room. "Obviously she was still upset from losing her Father, but she was looking forward to the journey, normally she drove everywhere. Her work took her all over the country, but always involved driving, so she saw this as a break."

"My Mother's well known, she decorates houses of famous musicians and people that have more money than sense, would you like to see a photograph?" I walked over to the magazine rack next to the sofa. I knew she was in the latest edition of *Design Monthly* and flicked through the pages until I found the section on her. I handed it over to Mayer and sat down again.

"Thanks Martha, that was the next question we were going to ask, if you had a recent photograph." He studied the picture hard and handed it over to Charlotte.

She looked at it then said "Mr. James, can you give us a description of what Meredith was wearing when she left?"

My mind drifted back to the conversation we'd had the day before, her teasing us about wearing glittery lilac trousers and shocking the solicitor. I hoped she had worn them, this would make it easier for people to spot her and come forward.

"She was wearing a black jacket, shirt and pale lilac linen trousers." My Father's words seemed light and frail, he looked over to me, knowing what was running through my head. A sense of loss hit me for the first time, I hadn't seen her that morning and the image of how I thought she would look started to fade from my mind.

"How tall is she and does she have any distinctive marks, Mr. James?" Mayer asked.

Father paused for awhile, I could see he was searching in his head for anything that would make her stand out in a crowd.

"She has green eyes, not hazel green, but the purest. Many people think she wears contact lenses, but they are her own colour. I would say she is about 5ft 2 inches, but I'm ashamed to say I don't know her exact height." He lowered his head not wanting to make eye contact with any of us.

Incensed by my Father's vagueness, I decided to correct him and take charge. "She is 157.5 cm tall to be precise and has no scars or blemishes on her face. She always wears a silver necklace of a fox and wears lilac in some way or other. She has shoulder length curly auburn hair, but you can see that from the photograph. What else do you want to know?" The irritation in my voice was becoming obvious. They both stared at me hard; I could see they were bemused by me, but I was used to that look.

"I'm sorry I have to ask this Mr. James," Mayer paused for a second, "but we have to ask these questions, could you tell me if you and your wife quarrelled the night before she left?"

I watched my Father's mouth intently as he said no and he gave me a look as to say *"Don't say one word"*. Mayer looked over at me; this was a time my face never let me down, the lack of expression hid a lie. I knew the truth, but would keep it locked inside me until I could find out more.

"Can you show me around the house Martha, perhaps there's something that may help us find where she is?" Charlotte got up and walked towards the door, "If that's ok with your dad?"

"That's a good idea," said Mayer. "I can continue filling in all the information with Mr. James."

"Ok," I said, "I've checked everything, but you're quite welcome, we can start in the dining room." I led her down the hallway still clutching the 'to do list', hoping to show her that she intended to come back.

"This is a lovely house, Martha, have you lived here long?" She was smiling and somehow I started to like her. Her face was fresh and obviously hadn't experienced the horrors other police officers witness; either that or she was good at disguising it. I decided I would call her Charlie after all.

"My parents moved here before I was born. They wanted to move further out of the city to be near the countryside, but not too far for my Dad to commute to work."

"How old are you, Martha, if you don't mind me asking?" She tipped her head to one side and her smile widened.

"I'm fifteen and before you say it, yes I know I look a lot older. Most people think I'm over eighteen, but it's my height, I'm more like my Dad and apparently I'm still growing. Would you like a drink, coffee or tea? I can go and make one whilst you're looking around."

There was something about her that I trusted, but I couldn't put my finger on it, perhaps it was because she reminded me of Lizzie.

"No, I'm fine thank you, Martha, I shan't take long. We'll have to go back to the station shortly and make a few enquiries and hopefully find where your Mother is. I'm sure she's ok, most people that are reported missing usually turn up." Her soft face seemed genuine and I wanted to believe her.

We spent the next half hour going through each room; she remarked on how beautiful my bedroom was and I explained to her about my Mother's love for that certain colour. Finally, Charlie asked if she could look at my Mother's studio to see if we'd missed any notes or letters she may have left. The studio was the one place I'd forgotten to check, but I didn't have a key as she always kept it locked if she was away. I left Charlie in the garden and rushed back up to the house. I could hear my Father still talking to Mayer and bolted into the room, I was out of breath and could barely get my words out.

"We forgot the studio," I panted. "Where are the keys?" Mayer was looking more serious and my Father was still pacing up and down the living room.

"She always keeps the keys on her, I'm not sure where the spare set are kept, Sara's just called and said she's not heard off her either." He looked ashen and his voice was merely a whisper.

"Well if it's ok with you, Mr. James, we can try and force the lock?" Mayer walked towards me, "I'll have a go, Martha, if you show me where it is."

"Charlie's in the garden where the studio is, I'll take you."

When we got outside Charlie was nowhere to be seen. I could see the studio door was wide open and realised she must have managed to break the lock. As we entered Charlie was looking at the sketches on the wall. The fabrics had all been stacked away on shelves and all her paints and brushes were nowhere to been seen.

"It was already open, Martha, your Mother must have forgotten to lock it." Charlie said.

This was impossible I thought, her studio was hers alone and she had total control of anyone entering it. She would never leave it unlocked and my heart sank as I realised that the morning she left, she couldn't have been thinking straight.

"Anything out of the ordinary?" Mayer asked while staring round the room.

"I'm not sure," I answered. "I wasn't allowed in here very often, but she brought me in here on Sunday. She was working on a new project and showed me some of the photos she'd taken."

I walked over to her desk and went to open the drawer expecting to find the photos there. This was where she had kept them, but when I looked they were gone.

"They're not here." I exclaimed "She must have taken them with her." I walked round the studio and stopped at the bookcase. Every book was neatly placed in alphabetical order and packed together so tight there was barely room for one more. Starting with A, 'Architecture of 18th Century Churches', and finishing with Z, 'Zoological Specimens in Victorian Times'. My fingers brushed along the bindings and I remembered her words about there being a fortune on these shelves. As my eyes got to the letter T, I noticed a gap where a book should have stood. What could have been there I thought? There were books called 'Trees of the British Isles' and 'Tapestries from Around the World', but what was the T that was missing? It was a large gap; therefore it must have been a heavy book and the shelf had slightly bowed from its weight.

"Right then, Martha" said Charlie as she checked the time on her watch, "if there's no more you can tell us we will have a quick chat with your Father and then go back to the station."

I decided not to tell them about the missing book, it probably wasn't relevant to them and they seemed keen to get back.

"Can I ask a question before you go, Mr. Mayer?" I said as he was walking towards the door.

"Of course." He turned round to look at me.

"Are you married?" I could see he was quite taken aback by my words.

"No, why do you ask?" he replied sharply.

"I just wondered, no reason." Charlie grinned at me and I had the feeling she knew what was running through my head, no wonder he was so overweight.

They had gone by the time I got back to the house, my Father was in the kitchen sat at the table. He was studying a small card and he passed it over to me.

"The police have given me this, Matty, it's the number for the missing persons bureau, apparently they can advise us what to do next, but we have to leave it 48 hours in case they come up with something."

He now had tears in his eyes and I wanted to hold him. My Mother had showed me many times how to put an arm around someone and I tried. I walked over to him and stiffly put my hand on his shoulder.

"They will find her Dad, everything will be ok."

If only I believed my own words.

CHAPTER 4

Lizzie had tried her best to help me pack, taking out the clothes I had neatly placed in my suitcase and replacing them with so called more suitable wear.

"You'll need your walking boots, Matty, there's nothing else to do round there."

She was still smiling, despite the fact I could barely speak to her. She'd asked my Father if I could stay with her parents, but he would have none of it, he said it was unfair on them and they'd done enough for us over the past year.

I looked at her as she walked round my bedroom, opening up drawers and taking out clothes. She was muttering to herself about how I needed to liven up my image and it was about time I bought something new. Her words seemed to fade into the distance and I remembered how she'd held my hand, day after day, never questioning my silence. She seemed to know when my thoughts would take me down dark corridors towards unopened doors. Time and time again I asked myself why she tolerated me, she could have the pick of so many other friends.

"Why are we friends Lizzie?" I asked as she folded up a t-shirt, "I'm nothing like you."

I stared down at what was once a comfort; the carpet no longer felt soft, but hard and coarse, like sand under my feet. Everything in my room seemed wrong and that one colour now made me feel sick, the photo of my parents had been turned face down on my dressing table, I never wanted to look at it again.

"It really doesn't matter why, Matty, it is the way it is. I could say it was your wicked sense of humour and joke telling." She was now grinning and held up a knitted scarf.

"It's summer stupid, I won't need that." I grabbed the scarf and put it back in the drawer.

"Well there are no bikinis in here. Don't worry Matty, no-one in Pendine will see your lily white flesh." She said laughing while holding up a pair of gloves.

I decided it was best to let her carry on, my mind had lost its way and my filing system had gone. It was a dark void, the thought of going back to Pendine and staying with my Grandmother was more than I could bear. "It will only be for a short while," my Father had said, but my Mother had uttered the same words.

"I've put some antihistamines in your case Matty, you know you sneeze at anything with four legs."

Lizzie closed the case and sat down on my bed looking at me with her wide blue eyes. This was true, my Father had wanted me to have a dog, he thought it would help with my so called *isolation problems*. Thankfully my eyes streamed and my asthma would go into overdrive if I came into contact with any fur. It did me a favour, animals were for people who showed love and compassion, this counted me out and I was grateful.

"You will keep in touch and let me know how you're getting on with the *Wicked Witch of Wales*?" she chuckled.

Lizzie lay back on my bed and I wondered if she could see the small patch of ceiling that the paint had missed; I had stopped looking.

"I will try," I said, but I knew this would be impossible.

Grandmother didn't believe in computers and getting a phone signal meant standing in a field with your hand up in the air, or walking to the seafront in the hope that a mast somewhere would pick up my SOS. I had decided that, once there, I would lock myself away until my Father came to collect me. People would recognise me and ask questions, so it would be safer if I stayed inside. No staring eyes or pointing fingers could get to me within the house, only her cold eyes and, hopefully, she would have gone blind through mourning.

Father had gone into town to sort out the last of his travel arrangements; as soon as he was back we would set off to Pendine.

He would not stay, as his flight was early the following day. Lizzie carried on chatting about what she would do while I was away. She'd been asked out by a boy at her school and had fallen in love, yet again. She fell in love with every boy who showed interest in her, but was convinced this one was somehow different.

"He wants to be a doctor," she exclaimed.

For the first time in days I felt amused and wondered if this one would end up being the heart surgeon.

"Does he have a Great Dane?" I asked, but then she went into great detail about how his mother bred poodles and entered them into Crufts.

"He's not the one for you Lizzie, it will probably last a week." She ignored my remarks and took out her phone to show me a photo of him.

"Don't you think he's gorgeous, Matty? Come on you have to admit he's got something?"

He's certainly got lots of spots.

"He's ok, if you like that sort of thing," I answered.

She grabbed my hand and squeezed it tightly, "Everything will be ok, Matty. Have you got Charlie's number just in case?"

I knew it well and nodded. "Her card is in my purse, have you got it?"

Lizzie smiled and squeezed my hand more tightly, "Yes, I've got it, but hopefully we won't need it. I'd best go as your Dad will be here soon."

She let go of my hand and I wondered if I would ever see her again. Then she put her arms around me and whispered in my ear, "You'll be back my lovely serious friend."

I could feel the warmth of her body and I didn't want her to let me go. She walked out of my bedroom looking back only once.

"Love you," she said, and then was gone.

I sat alone with my suitcase beside me, soon I would be on that journey back to Wales. Father said we would travel on the motorway, it was quicker and we should be in Pendine by early evening.

On the way staring out of the window, I saw a lorry carrying sheep, no doubt on their way to the slaughterhouse, their faces crammed up against the wooden slats, desperate to get out. The parallels of this vision were akin to my own position. My Father tried to have a conversation with me in-between cursing other drivers who overtook him at great speed. As each motorway junction passed, his conversation dwindled and eventually silence fell in the car. We were near Swansea, and I knew that in the next hour, I would be standing outside that house. The white house on the hill over looking Pendine Sands, its walls battered with the sea breeze and rain that had taken its toll on every window pane. I thought about begging him one more time to turn back, but nothing came from my mouth. The sun had disappeared behind the clouds and large drops of water landed on the windscreen; we would soon be in St Cleares. Shop windows displaying posters, faded and torn by the past few months sun, asking the public if they'd seen this person. It would be my Mother's face, a photo taken some years back with her red hair tied back. Why had they never used the one I'd given them? Mine showed her wearing lilac, her hair down and laughing with that infectious smile, but they had chosen a portfolio shot from a magazine. She looked serious and her eyes less green, it could have been anyone's mother, certainly not mine. I decided to close my eyes for the rest of the journey and time the sound of the windscreen wipers; they quickened up as the force of the rain became stronger. Losing count at 1,008, I drifted into a sleep, taking me back to the press conference…

As soon as we sat down, the flashing started, cameras too large for some to hold were ready to capture flowing tears from a grieving family. My face remained the same as it always did and I know this worried my Father.

"It's best that you let me do the talking, Matty," he said. What he really meant was *"People won't understand why your eyes aren't swollen and red like mine."*

Two microphones sat on the table, one for my Father and the other for Chief Inspector Spalding. Now two police forces were involved, but Dyfed-Powys Police thought that as she had gone missing in Wales, then they should take control, although neither had yet come up with any answers. Charlie was still there, sat next to me, holding my hand under the table. It had gone from a missing person's case to a possible murder enquiry within a week. After endless questions thrown at me, Charlie had realised I was not like other girls. She'd been allocated to look after me by West Midlands Police in case I came out with something inappropriate and because I was still classed as a minor. I'd sworn at the forensic team for not leaving my bedroom tidy, my outburst only controlled by her offering to help me put it back in some order once they had finished.

"I'm Chief Inspector Spalding of Dyfed-Powys Police and I'd like to thank you all for attending today. We would like to appeal to the general public if they have any knowledge of the whereabouts of Meredith James."

Now the cameras were clicking fast, the noise stifling the sounds of my Father's sobs.

"Meredith was last seen on Monday morning, the CCTV shows her disembarking a train at Tenby station at approximately 13:40 pm. The footage shows her leaving the platform towards the car park where she was due to catch a taxi to Pendine, although we are unable to confirm if this occurred."

Charlie squeezed my hand tighter as if this would help in someway. Spalding continued to give a description of what my Mother was wearing and held up a photo to the cameras.

"If any of the general public have seen Meredith James, can they contact either Dyfed-Powys Police or West Midlands Police on the numbers that will be given out at the end of this conference. I know that Mr. James would like to say a few words now."

All eyes turned towards my Father. He seemed in no fit state to speak and grabbed the glass of water that was in front of him. A few minutes past and he finally spoke.

"Meredith, if you can see this, then please come home." Tears were streaming down his face and his voice was no longer that of a confident lawyer. "Your family misses you every minute of the day and wants you back home with us. If anyone out there has seen or knows where my wife is, then I beg you to contact the police;" by now his words were incoherent.

Journalists now shifted their attention to me, hoping I would turn into an emotional wreck so they could catch it on camera and rush back to their office for tomorrow's front page. Disappointing them, I sat silent, counting how many were in the room and wondering why there were so few women.

"As you can imagine this is a deeply distressing situation for the James family." Spalding took over. "We thank you for your co-operation and I would ask that you give the family some privacy at this difficult time. The number will appear on your screen."

It was then the questions started, they rose from their seats all at once, voices getting louder by the second, each trying to beat each other in the race to get their questions answered.

"Martha, is there anything you want to say?" One journalist said, sweat pouring from his face as he thrust a recorder towards me.

Charlie whispered in my ear, "Let's go." She put her hand on my shoulder expecting me to stand, but I was transfixed by this circus. "Martha, come on," her voice now louder trying to drown out the sounds in front of me. I felt a hand on my shoulder again, this time firmer.

"Martha… MARTHA…"

I heard the screeching of brakes and woke with a sudden jolt, my eyes tried to focus on where we were.

"Are we here?" I said, rubbing my face and looking around.

"No, Matty, I nearly ran over a bloody rabbit, missed it by an inch."

I could see now we were on a small country lane, overgrown hedges were either side and a seagull was flying high above the car. Its cries made me realise the sea was near and so was she. It was the road into Pendine and we were a few minutes away.

"Let's turn back, please take me home." I turned towards my Father and put my hand on the steering wheel.

"You know we can't, Matty, we've been through this a hundred times already."

He switched the engine back on and we carried on down the lane. I could see the house in the distance. Standing high up on the hill facing out to sea, whitewashed stone, it stood alone. We took a left turn and drove slowly down the hill; no words were shared, just the sound of that single seagull. He seemed to be following us, swooping low down towards the car.

Serves him right if it gets hit.

The car turned up the driveway; the conifers that lined either side were now overgrown. My Grandfather used to neatly cut them, framing the gravel before it opened wide to the front of the house. As we pulled up to the large wooden door, I could see weeds sprouting through the gravel. Where red roses once climbed against the brickwork now stood brown sticks desperately trying to climb for their life. The window boxes no longer blazed with colour and the large brass doorbell was tarnished with neglect.

The windows either side of the door were dark with dust and where white lace once hung there were dingy remnants of net. One single light shone from the window on the left as a lamp tried its best to remind the world that someone lived there.

I looked up towards the roof, where the seagull had now landed, its eyes firmly fixed on us. It pecked at the moss growing between the roof tiles, then began screeching and spreading its wings. It was telling her we had arrived. The hallway light went on with a dim glow. There was no turning back, I fumbled for my purse and took out a card; it was Charlie's number and I held it close to my chest.

"I've a feeling I'm going to need this," I muttered to myself.

CHAPTER 5

We stayed in the car, the windscreen wipers still thrashing away at the relentless rain.

"We best get out," my Father said.

He opened the car door and got out; the rain battered down soaking him within seconds. I stayed there watching the water tumble from the windscreen like a river: minutes passed. He was standing in the doorway, waving at me to follow him, but my mind was racing. I wondered if I could lock myself in and stay here forever, or turn the ignition key on and drive the car forward into the walls of the house. Any fate seemed better than staying with a woman who barely knew me. I could see the frustration on his face and he waved again, so I took a deep breath and opened the car door, running towards him, the rain streaming down my face turning my long black hair into lank strands.

The door was ajar as we entered the hallway. I expected to find her waiting, but it was empty. Long and dimly lit, there were doors leading off from each side and a musty smell hit me like a brick. Plants stood on tables along its walls and their leaves were brown, gasping for water. Large gilt mirrors hung on each side, bouncing back dim light to each other, giving the appearance of an endless dark tunnel. Along one wall stood a table, strewn with tourist leaflets. A brass bell, once highly polished, sat dully next to them with *Ring for Assistance* engraved on it. The large grandfather clock ticked away, its previously shining face was now deeply pitted with rust. The moon and stars that once sat enamelled in all their glory, were now barely visible. Its hands still ticked away, the pendulum swinging backwards and forward as it always had. When I was much younger I would run as fast as I could, passing the clock

39

without a glance, in case its hands leapt out and choked the breath from me. It no longer seemed threatening just old and tired, wanting to be left alone and its ticking eventually allowed to fade away.

"Dylis, are you there?" my Father called.

I hid behind him, my eyes closed desperately trying to will no-one to answer. The door at the end of the hallway slowly opened and a voice quietly spoke.

"You're late, come through."

We entered the room. Clinging on to the back of my Father's jacket not wanting to let go, I opened my eyes. She was sat perched on a wingback chair, studying a book about seabirds of Wales. I expected to see an elderly lady full of grief, one that had neglected herself as much as the house in which she lived. Instead sat an elegant and small woman, her once flame-red hair was now grey, tied neatly into a ponytail. A large black velvet bow held it in place and I remembered the beauty she once had. Her high cheekbones and sculptured features had worn well with age. Her nails were perfectly manicured and each finger wore a ring that my Grandfather had made for her. Silver bangles hung from each wrist and jangled softly as she beckoned us in.

"Only a few minutes," my Father said, checking his watch and taking off his coat.

"You've grown, Martha." She looked towards me, studying me hard with her hazel eyes.

"Come sit down, I will go and make a drink, you both must be thirsty."

As she rose she seemed to gain height, like a swan extending its graceful neck with pride.

"I can't stay long, Dylis, I have got to get back and make a few calls before my flight. I'll go and get Martha's case from the car." He left me alone with her, my hair still dripping on the carpet.

"Lost your tongue, eh?" she said with a wry smile.

"I… err…" stammering to get my words out, "I'm… err… sorry… errrm… how are you Grandma?"

"As well as could be expected, thank you. Aren't you going to give your Grandma a kiss? You weren't at the funeral and it's been awhile."

She walked over to me, tilting her cheek to one side in anticipation. I quickly kissed her, smelling the powder that masked her age.

"That's better." Her smile soon disappeared and she sat back down. The room was cold; the oppressive summer heat had struggled to enter.

Father came back in, carrying my case, and still wet from the rain. He glanced towards me and shook his hair.

"It's still throwing it down out there, but the sun is desperately trying to break through. Shall I take Martha's case up, Dylis?"

I was hoping that Lizzie had packed me some warm clothes, if each room was as cold as this one, I would need them.

"She can have Meredith's old room. I've made it ready if you want to take her things up."

My Mother's room, I thought. Whenever we'd stayed in the past we'd used one of the guest rooms. I didn't even know where about in the house her old bedroom was. She'd never shown me.

"Follow me," she said, leaving us both wondering where she would take us.

We climbed the large staircase, clutching on to the banister I looked up, it seemed endless, twisting and turning until we eventually stopped on the third floor. I'd never been up here, never allowed to see higher than the second floor. She stopped outside a cream door, its handle painted with flowers and crazed with age.

"Here we are, Stuart, go right in and get Martha settled, I'll see you before you go."

With that she turned and went downstairs, the sound of her silver bracelets fading in the distance.

"Right, let's get you sorted, Matty." He turned the handle and we walked in. I felt a rush of curiosity upon entering a room that belonged to my Mother. Perhaps I might find some answers to the many questions I never had time to ask.

The room was much warmer than the one that we had met my Grandmother in; its window was facing the back of the house to the garden. A brass bed stood in the corner adorned with a colourful handmade quilt. Against another wall stood a highly carved dressing table supporting a wooden mirror on a stand. There was an old teddy bear leaning against it; its one eye gone and stuffing was sprouting from its arm.

"This must have been Mom's." I rushed towards the bear and held it high in the air putting it against my face, desperately hoping to smell the perfume she once wore.

"Well, I'm sure your Mother would have wanted you to have it, we can ask your Grandma when we go down."

"No." My words now bitter. "I want nothing from her, and besides the police would have been through everything in the room and no doubt covered it with fingerprint powder."

I placed the bear back down on the dressing table and had another look around, hoping to find something else that belonged to her. A large wardrobe stretched the length of one wall. It had three doors, two of which were open with keys hanging from their locks and one firmly shut. I put my head inside and they were empty, apart from hangers, waiting for my clothes to be neatly arranged in order. The smell of moth balls oozed from the old wood.

"I have to go in a few minutes, Matty." He walked towards me, putting his arms out as if to hold me.

"Two weeks, that's all, angel, you can dream about our holiday while I am away."

"You will come back, won't you?"

"Of course I'll be back, please try and be polite to her. She's been through a rough time like us, not only did she lose her husband, but her daughter as well. It can't have been easy."

"Well she hardly looks like some mourning widow! Don't you think she looks as if she has had a facelift?"

"Martha, you know yourself that faces don't always reflect what people's true emotions are. Please, just for me try, and make an effort, it's only for a short time. Perhaps you can offer to help clean the place up a bit, she's obviously let things go."

I thought for awhile, "Ok, just for you I will try, but don't expect miracles!"

I decided I would unpack after he'd gone. I wanted to spend every precious minute with him. What if his plane crashed? What if he was involved in some terrible traffic accident on the way to the airport? Every 'what if' entered my head and the thought of being an orphan started to consume me.

We closed the door behind us and went back downstairs; she was there in the hallway staring into one of the mirrors. Her fingers caressing her hair, patting each loose strand and putting it in place, she could see us standing behind her, but carried on preening herself.

"You off now then?" she said, not turning, but gazing at our reflection.

"Yes, Dylis, Martha said she would help you around the house while I am away, didn't you?" He glanced towards me and she spun around, the silver dancing on her wrists.

"Oh, how lovely, that's very kind of you, Martha. There's certainly lots of jobs to do and I'm sure you don't want to be going out and about, do you?"

The subdued light of the hallway cast a shadow across her face and, for one moment I thought her eyes had turned black, no longer looking elegant, but a memory from my nightmares.

"Oh, and by the way, Stuart, I've had a call from Chief Inspector Spalding, he'd tried to call you this afternoon." Father quickly fumbled in his pocket for his phone.

"Damn it, no signal. I can't even see if I've got a missed call never mind a voicemail. What did he want?"

I backed away and sat at the foot of the stairs, no longer wanting to spend my last few minutes with someone who had put us in a position where news of my Mother had become second-hand.

"They're scaling down the team and taking officers off the case, apparently it's standard after twelve months, he thought we should know." Her tone seemed matter of fact as she walked towards the front door, opening it wide, waiting for him to leave.

The rain had now stopped and I could see steam rising from the warm earth outside, creating a summer fog. He looked at me, his face trying to say sorry without words, but I couldn't bear it. I turned and ran up the stairs, never looking back once. She was gone and now he would be gone too, I felt totally alone. My Mother was last year's news, a statistic in a police file, soon a black stamp would be impressed upon her file: "*Archived*".

CHAPTER 6

Sunlight streamed through the bedroom window, sending dust particles floating in the air of the room that once belonged to my Mother. As they landed and collected on my tongue, I could taste the age of the room. I pressed my body hard against the door, my head rhythmically banging back against the wood. Was this to be my prison for the next two weeks? I visualised a hatch in the door where my food would be passed. Slops and Dickensian gruel would be my fuel and perhaps, if I was lucky, she might give me water. My suitcase lay on the bed, disappearing amongst a sea of coloured patchwork: from reds, greens and yellows to pinks, purples and browns, each square neatly stitched, but not one showed the colour my Mother loved. In fact, there was no hint of lilac in the room, the carpet a deep maroon, clashing with the rose print wallpaper. The heavy beige curtains were pulling at the rail that desperately tried to hold them from falling; it was a complete visual assault. This was a room of chaos, no thought of design and no sign that my Mother had been here. I walked towards the wardrobe, the two doors open waiting for my clothes to be hung. The third door was firmly closed, it had no key and I tugged at the handle furiously; the irritation of not being able to open it made me kick out. It rattled and shook with the force of my foot, causing it to sway towards me. I quickly steadied it with my hands, praying she hadn't heard from downstairs. I waited in silence, expecting to hear the sound of silver coming up the stairs, but there was nothing. Now grateful for being on the third floor, I lay on the bed and checked my phone.

It showed 18:30, but nothing else; the battery was dying, so I threw it across the room, watching it bounce like a pebble across the carpet. Other than time checking it was now useless to me. I hoped it would drown in the carpet. It was yet another thing to let me down and I felt punished. Perhaps in a previous life I had been cruel, tormenting souls and reigning down terror on all I met and karma was now dealing its hand. Realising that my self-wallowing thoughts were not going to help me unpack, I opened my case. Lizzie had neatly folded an array of clothes; T-shirts, jeans and jumpers with a bottle of sun lotion lying on the top. The thought of me bathing on the sands, waiting for my white skin to turn golden was ridiculously bizarre, and she knew it. If I could have smiled, I would have. Next to the lotion was my inhaler and antihistamines, which I placed on the dressing table next to the old teddy, its one eye watching me walk round the room, seeming to take in everything I touched. Was this the room my Mother would laugh and dance around, in her carefree spirit bouncing off each wall? It offered no such comfort to me, there was nothing to lighten my spirits or inspire a dance. The old wooden hangers rattled as I hung up my clothes, all colour co-ordinated and in order, starting with summer wear and ending with waterproof jackets and jumpers. My walking boots were placed underneath alongside some flip flops that Lizzie must have smuggled in. Drawer after drawer was pulled out in the hope I might find something else that belonged to her, but all I discovered were scented drawer liners and the odd dead moth. Every imperfection of the room gnawed at me, the torn wallpaper longed to be stripped and replaced with lilac. How could she have stayed in a room like this?

The heat was suffocating, so I decided to try and open the sash window, hoping the fresh air might cleanse the room; many months must have passed since anyone had entered. Apart from detectives and people wearing white forensic suits, I was the only one to be here since she had gone. They would have picked over the bones of her life looking for anything that would lead them to find out where she was. Any relevant personal belongings would have been placed in transparent bags and taken away, leaving nothing apart from the old teddy who was still staring at me. Our house had been thoroughly searched, my once perfect bedroom had been stripped and analysed. Hair and fibres were taken, shining lilac threads in glass jars and anything that had been touched by us. The computer had been seized in the hope they would find some explanation for her disappearance. Perhaps a sordid email to a long lost lover?

I tugged at the window, with every bit of strength I could muster, but it was unforgiving. It was completely jammed; the glass quivering in its frame looked fragile, I could hear a creak as if it might splinter at any moment. I would ask her to open it later, even if it meant forcing it with a knife; the thought of sleeping in this vacuum flask was too much to cope with.

Soon I was coughing and felt the familiar tightness in my chest. I gasped for breathe and grabbed my inhaler from the dressing table. The taste hit the back of my throat, it had entered my body at the right time and soon my breathing would be back to normal. My head began to pound and with trembling hands I sat back on the bed, needing the after effects to wear off before going downstairs. If she saw me shaking, she would think me weak, blame my Father and accuse him of smothering me in cotton wool.

I hadn't eaten anything since breakfast and I was beginning to feel hungry. Realising I could not avoid her any longer, I decided to go downstairs. As I got nearer to the bottom floor, the smell of burnt toast filled the air. The kitchen was at the front of the house, divided by a large workstation and spacious enough for twenty guests to be comfortable. My Grandfather loved to chat to those who stayed while my Grandmother served breakfast that was the talk of the area. Each table would be covered with a crisp white linen cloth, shining with silver cutlery ready to be used by an eager traveller.

As I entered, I noticed there was only one table and chair, placed near the window, a plain crumpled cloth thrown across without care. She was stood next to the cooker, her arms folded, humming to herself a discordant tune.

"You took longer than I thought. I can cook some more if you want?" She thrust the plate towards me and told me to sit down.

Pulling the chair out and realising that this might be the only food I would get tonight, I slowly ate each piece wondering how long it had been since she had cooked for someone. It tasted bitter; perhaps she had laced it with some toxic plant from the garden? I recalled the time my Mother pulled me away from a patch of foxgloves saying that one bite of them could stop your heart. I am not sure if this was the truth, but it frightened me enough to stay away from them. There were two options in front of me; I could try and engage in a conversation with a woman who seemed full of rage, or avoid eye contact and attempt to look out of a dirty window. As I fumbled with the torn nets in the hope I may see daylight the 'No Vacancy' sign fell to the floor.

"Leave it alone!" she bellowed. I quickly picked it up and placed it back in the window.

"So, tell me Martha, what's life been like in Birmingham for you? You seem to have grown into a woman in such a short space of time." She pulled a stool from behind the work station and sat opposite me. So, now was the time to be interrogated, I thought. I knew it wouldn't be long before I was grilled about my life and no doubt she would ask me about my Father. His words rang through my head, be civil and make an effort.

"I've finished my exams," was all that I could say, my mouth still dry from the burnt offerings.

"So, no boyfriend yet?" She whispered the words, barely opening her mouth.

"No, I'm not interested and need to concentrate on my studies."

"You must be tired, Martha. I will clear up if you want to shower and settle yourself in." She got up, snatching my plate away before the last crumb had entered my mouth.

"Yes I am, thank you."

A sense of relief came over me, no more questions for tonight, perhaps tomorrow she would grill me on my life and the small circle of people within it.

As I left the kitchen, I said "My window won't open. Have you got anything I can ease it up with? I think it's jammed."

"Ah, I meant to get that fixed ages ago along with other jobs. I've got a fan you can have for tonight and tomorrow we can sort something out. I'll bring it up later, there's a bathroom opposite your room you can use."

She turned her back to me and made her way to the sink, her humming started up again. It was a tune I thought I'd heard before, somewhere in my distant past. Perhaps my Mother had sung it to me, I couldn't remember, but its mournful melody brought back memories.

The bathroom was stark, but was sufficient to keep me clean. A cracked mirror hung above the sink, making my face distorted. If I stood in a certain position the crack almost gave me the impression of a smile. I stood there moving my face around while the shower water ran. I enjoyed this experience and wished I could carry the mirror around with me, showing people the possibilities of a different Martha.

After I had showered, I returned to my room; the heat now had become suffocating and sweat started to collect on my brow. It seemed pointless that I had made myself clean only to return to a sweltering oven. It wasn't long before there was a knock at the door.

"Here's the fan, hope you have a good night's sleep."

I opened the door expecting her to be standing there, but she was gone. I hadn't heard her come up or return downstairs. The only explanation I could come up with was that she must have taken her bangles off. The fan came as a slight relief, but the dust that had settled now spun across the room, its years of lying in corners now gave it wings to fly into my lungs.

Lying on the bed, my inhaler between my mouth, I was pleasantly surprised at how soft the mattress was. My body sank deep within its coils and my eyes became heavy. The rhythmic whirring of the fan sent me to sleep. No dreams came to me that night and the only sound I heard was the bleep of my mobile. The battery must be completely dead, I would recharge it in the morning.

CHAPTER 7

"Smile before you can run
You will dance with my midnight
Before the rising sun"

The hours without nightmares had recharged my batteries; I'd set myself a list of things to do: washing the nets in the kitchen would be first on my list, the summer breeze would dry them while I cleaned the windows. I'd worked out precisely minute by minute how long it would take and I had calculated that one hour and ten minutes should see it done. Plugging in my phone I looked to see if the noise I'd heard in the night could have been a message, but there was nothing, I had desperately hoped it might have been my Father, but he would no doubt still be in mid-flight, travelling over some exotic ocean, his thoughts no longer on me. It was still showing no signal and I realised it was pointless looking in the future; apart from checking the time and counting down the days, it was of little use to me.

It was Friday, 8.00am, and the longest I had slept in many months, the thought of my drugged supper came back to me for a second. My pulse was normal, so I dismissed the idea as quickly as it had appeared. A note had been placed on the hall table *'Gone to Tenby to stock up, won't be long.'* There was no *'Dear Martha'* or *'from your loving Grandma'*. This was good news, I could start to investigate the house, always being mindful to listen out for the sound of her car returning. When I had stayed with my Mother in the past we were given a guest room on the first floor. Father was always too busy with his work to come, but as I grew older, I realised this was an excuse. I wondered if the room was still the same, two basic single beds, a chest of drawers beside them with a Bible on each. All the guest rooms were stark, but clean; occasionally a vase of red roses would be put out for a special guest. We were never special, not one flower was ever cut for our arrival. They had prided themselves on winning four stars one year in a travel magazine. "God knows how!" my Father had exclaimed. Grandfather would endlessly be fixing doors or showers that a guest had grumbled about, but they always returned each year. Now a shadow of its former self, I doubted anyone would want to stay here.

The floor groaned underneath me as I stood outside our old room. When my feet were smaller and I was younger and the groans seemed more threatening, my Mother would hold my hand before we entered, whispering words of reassurance. It was just an old house full of old people, both tired and weary. The warmth of her hand was suddenly replaced by the coldness of the brass handle. It turned and was unforgiving. I turned it again, but it did not want me to enter. In frustration, I clasped both my hands and pushed. The lock rattled back at me mocking my attempts. As I walked away to try the next door the heavy smell of lavender crept up behind me. I closed my eyes not wanting to turn around for fear of seeing the ghost of an elderly guest who had died slowly of some horrible death, while my Grandmother sipped tea and combed her silver hair. The next handle wouldn't even turn and the smell of lavender was becoming even stronger. Fear and frustration made me kick out at the final locked door, my head now spinning with the smell of a plant that should remain in a garden.

Realising it was a pointless task trying any other room, I went into the kitchen; the solitary table was still there and a box of cereal had been left for me, not a named brand, but some budget sawdust that felt like razor blades on each swallow. I washed my bowl and set about getting down the nets; the chair wobbled underneath me as I unhooked each rusty clip. Now the windows were completely bare I could finally see the world outside; the flowers in the window boxes were neglected like everything else and had shrivelled in the sun. Where bees would once bathe on pollen, now crawled ugly insects, all fighting for survival and battling for what little soil remained. A large seagull flew down and landed on the box; he tugged at the bugs, pulling them high up into the air, throwing his head back and swallowing in one go. All seagulls looked the same, white snowy heads with grey wings, their yellow eyes blinking at every movement. This one had a familiarity, could it be the same one that had followed us to the house? I had only been here a few hours, yet ridiculous irrational thoughts were entering my head. I must get a grip or I would go mad.

Banging the window hard I shouted, "Go away!" he turned his head towards me, ignoring my words, as another beetle disappeared in one swallow. I screamed at it to flee and, with that he took flight, letting out a final shriek of disapproval before disappearing.

The nets sank deep into the hot soapy water, my bare hands reddened as they scrubbed away in desperation to get them clean. Soon the white lace returned back to its former glory and perhaps when they were dried the holes would be less noticeable.

The large kitchen door that led out into the garden had been left ajar. Holding the dripping nets, I stepped outside, knowing it was unlikely to resemble anything I had remembered. It used to be my Grandfather's pride and joy, always making sure it was a paradise and haven for guests to sit and relax in. There would be benches dotted around the edge, travellers reading books and sipping Earl Grey tea on white wrought iron tables, the lawn with tramlines carefully mowed and mapped out with precision, like a runway of grass. Either side, large beech hedges made a luscious green wall, high enough for privacy, but still allowing the afternoon sun to rest on all who stayed there.

Each long blade of grass still sodden from yesterday's rain was now battling for space, strangling each other in a frenzy for light, making a carpet of green chaos where once was order. Dandelions poked their yellow heads between each blade, as stinging nettles tried with all their might to pierce through my jeans. The hedges were overgrown, casting dark shadows across what used to be a lawn. A large wooden shed leant lazily to one side, previously containing my Grandfather's gardening tools and the remnants of his machinery for making jewellery. No doubt she had probably sold it all, not wanting to be reminded of the days in Tenby when he was happy and creative.

Next to it stood the washing line; the stepping stones leading up to it had long since gone. I had no option but to wade through the heavy grass. Pegging up the nets, my eyes gazed down towards the end of the garden where, past the broken benches and tables, stood a tree. I could not recall seeing it before, maybe because as a child I was not allowed to venture further than 3ft from the house; the grounds were not for me to play in. The tree stood about 30ft high, its branches stretching out trying to touch the hedges on either side.

I wandered towards it, the grass slowing my pace and making my legs feel heavy. As I ran my fingers across the flaking bark, woodlice scuttled and hurried to find refuge. Moss and lichens grew amongst its peeling layers making it their home. The twigs felt brittle, snapping between my fingers, crumbling in my hand and leaving a dusty residue. Dead leaves lay at its base, curled and brown, rotting in the grass that grew around it. On the end of each branch were small dried flowers, like tiny pieces of torn tissue paper. The tree was full of decay and, like the rest of the house, it should be chopped down to make way for things that wanted to live.

In the distance I heard the rumble of an engine and a car approaching; she must be back. Retracing my steps in the trodden down grass, I returned to the house to find her standing in the kitchen doorway. In the cold light of day I could see her true skin. I wondered if she smoked, as each line above her lips sat deep and twisted. Resting on each side of her eyes were the feet of crows. Max-Factor had tried to soften them to a sparrow's footprints. From the swan I had seen the previous night now stood a hawk, her nose was sharper, slightly beaked and ready to peck. She was wearing a tailored blue suit and black patent shoes, hardly the attire for walking the aisles of a supermarket.

Glancing at me briefly she muttered, "You slept well I gather, come and help me get the groceries from the car."

She turned, leaving me to wonder how she could have known about my hours of sleep, after all I hadn't seen her since the night before. How did she not know my mind hadn't wandered down dark hallways opening up doors full of nightmares.

"I've washed the nets and put them out to dry," was all I responded, as I knew she had no interest in me, my life or anyone else apart from herself.

"Good," she said sharply turning back round to me, "that's one job out of the way. Now come and help me unload the groceries."

As I followed her to the car, this small woman in front of me seemed to step without sound, not even when her feet touched the gravel did any noise come from those patent shoes. As we unpacked the car it became quite obvious that her shopping spree had been for herself and not me, apart from a box of cheap cereal, one loaf of bread and a small amount of cheese, everything else would be used to pamper herself. From face moisturisers to nail varnish, all the bags were full of luxuries to hide her age. There was one extra bag, which she insisted on carrying herself, it was rammed full of bird seed, no doubt for the seagull who was now sat back on the roof.

As I placed the solitary cheese in the fridge, the cold icy air hit my lungs; it looked lost on an empty shelf like me.

"I was wondering if it would be ok if I could have a look in Grandfather's shed? If the lawn mower is still there, perhaps I could cut the grass for you?"

The thought of pushing a rusty old machine across the green jungle filled me with dread; however it was a small price to pay to be away from her cold stare.

A red flame seemed to burn deep in her eyes; she let go of the bag of bird seed and hurled it across the tiled floor sending seeds into every inch of the kitchen.

"I don't want you touching anything that belonged to him! I have already arranged for someone to come out tomorrow to look at the garden and see what needs doing." She pulled out a compact from her handbag pouting to check her lipstick was still in place.

"You can clear this mess up." She walked towards the kettle, her feet no longer silent as she broke the sea of seeds underneath her.

"I didn't mean to upset you, I just thought I could try and cut the lawn, it's grown so high and I would like to sit out there and maybe do some painting."

She put the compact back in her bag sealing the Chanel clasp firmly.

"Oh, and by the way, I will get him to look at your bedroom window, while he's here."

Him I thought, I couldn't believe she was now willing to pay anybody to tidy the garden that had been left neglected for so long. Perhaps she intended to sell the place, now the will had been sorted and everything was in her name. I picked up the broom that was sat in the corner and started to sweep the seeds into a pile.

"Are you thinking about selling up?"

"Never," she snapped. I watched the flames rise in her eyes then die down to a flicker; her face softened slightly, remnants of the graceful bird came back and her voice became softer. "I'm going into the living room, you can join me when you have finished clearing this mess up. I would like to know more about your life in Birmingham."

I felt a sigh of relief as she left me alone, the thought of clearing up was a much better proposition than continuing a conversation with her. After I had inspected the floor for any solitary offending seed, I decided to go into the garden to see if the nets had dried. Holding them close against my cheek I was transported back to Sundays at home and my Mother singing at all things lilac on the line.

The old wood shed creaked in the heat and I decided to see if it was open. There was no key or lock on the door, just a small latch that had rusted over. To my surprise, his garden tools were still in there, the grass mower lay covered in cobwebs, but still looked in good working order. All of his machinery had gone, no doubt sold at an auction to buy more makeup. Leaning up against one wall was a bike. I recognised it by the basket sitting between the handle bars:

it was my Mother's. She had told me how she would ride down to the sea front at Pendine when she was younger. Sometimes she would ride to Laugharne to see Sara, her red hair blowing in the sea breeze, with not a care in the world. Apart from the teddy bear in my bedroom this was the only thing I'd seen so far that belonged to her, not only had she disappeared, but so had anything connected to her.

I tugged at it, pulling the front wheel towards me. Spiders ran for freedom from between its spokes and its red handlebars saw the sun for the first time in years. Climbing on to the saddle, I remembered how small my Mother was, my legs overhung the pedals like a giant. A tingling feeling went through my whole body, small electric shock waves went through my arms as I held onto the handlebars. This feeling of exhilaration was one I had never experienced and I cried out. I felt somehow different, strong and at one with the metal. The two flat tyres could be easily solved, somewhere in the shed must be a pump.

"What are you doing!"

She was standing behind me, blocking the exit from the shed door.

"Errr... I was just... errr... I was just looking to see if the lawnmower was still here and found Mom's old bike."

"How dare you go round snooping without asking!" She grabbed my shoulder tugging hard and pulling me away from the handlebars.

I loathed everything about this woman, her fingers dug deep into my shoulders taking away that connection in a split second.

"Well, I'm so sorry Grandma, forgive me for trying to do you a favour," I said sarcastically. "I'll tell Dad when he calls that you didn't want any help after all."

Power surged through my veins and I fixed my eyes on her; not blinking or showing any sense of fear, I waited for her to speak. What seemed like minutes passed before she finally opened her mouth.

"Err... There's no need to say anything to your Father. I've asked someone to come out later and look at your bedroom window, he can take a look at the bike as well." Her voice had now softened and her hands were trembling.

"Thank you," I said brusquely, "I can ride out on it when it's fixed."

Her face paled until almost transparent.

"You will be seen, people will know who you are." Finally she looked worried and I bathed in her anxiety.

"I'll deal with that and, by the way, I'm going to walk into Pendine this afternoon."

The brief seconds of sitting on my Mother's bike had given me an inner strength; freedom would soon be mine.

Leaving her standing in the garden, her mouth wide open, I returned to the house. From now on things were going to be different, no longer would I be a prisoner in this hell hole.

CHAPTER 8

I'd tied my hair back and found a baseball cap that Lizzie had packed, it suited her more than me. She could wear anything as it never detracted from her beauty. Looking more like a boy who had never seen the sun, I made my way down the hill to Pendine front. The road was silent apart from my walking boots rhythmically pounding the ground and a single male cricket calling to his mate somewhere in the hedgerows. It was the height of the holiday season and, soon, the sound of laughing children would be near, excited and chattering about paddling in the sea. Their mothers would be loud, shrieking at them to not wander too far from their view. They would lounge lazily back on hired deck chairs, desperate to gain a real tan rather than one that came from a spray can. Houses either side of the road proudly showed off their tended gardens, pampas grass swayed gently with the slight afternoon breeze. I'd left my Grandmother to eat on her own, not telling her what time I would get back. Money wasn't a problem for me, Father had made sure of that. From now on I would buy what I wanted and eat whenever I felt like it.

As I turned round the bend of the final slope of the hill, I spotted an elderly lady leaning on her gate. Her tight grey curls had been recently set, perfectly tiny Swiss rolls on a plump round face. She was talking softly to a postman, her Welsh accent made it difficult to understand what she was saying. They watched me walk past them, pausing only to smile briefly before continuing to chatter. The first test had been passed, they hadn't given me that glaring look of recognition.

Maybe my time here won't be as bad as I first thought, or perhaps they just don't watch TV.

The sea was on the horizon, vivid blue with white foam horses riding the waves. Gulls cried as they swooped and soared, waiting for a crumb to be dropped from a careless child. Suddenly, a sense of unease came over me, I felt as if I was being followed. It was then I heard the soft patter of steps coming up behind me. I quickly turned, my hands clenched ready to flail out, but there was no one.

Stop being so paranoid, Martha, it must be the echo of your own feet! My own feet don't sound like a patter, this is softer... Oh come on, I must a get a grip.

Taking a deep breath, I convinced myself it must be the postman going up a garden path to deliver letters, he was probably already well behind. Relieved I wasn't being shadowed, I continued on my way.

The peacefulness of the lane was broken as I reached the bottom of the hill. Cars were parked nose to tail, children were tugging the hands of their parents excited and desperate to splash in the salty water. Red-faced mothers with pushchairs looked like donkeys overladen with cool boxes, blankets and towels, their husbands walking in front oblivious of the heavy load being trawled behind them.

The air was full of holiday excitement, summer was here for those who had escaped the city and they were determined to enjoy it. Seven miles of sandy beach stretched before my eyes, where men raced cars and speed records had been broken, along with the bones of some of those who'd tried in an effort to be the best. The sea front wall acted as a leaning post for the elderly, they gazed out pointing to small boats bobbing up and down and wishing they could sail on them. It was a small resort, supplying a large caravan site with basic needs. A launderette, small supermarket and fish and chip shop was all that was required. The beach itself would entertain all those who stayed here. A pub stood on the corner, its old wooden benches supporting the locals who sat and chatted about how busy the holiday season was. Buckets and spades danced outside the gift shop, tied with string and longing for a child to come and pick them. The cafe that quenched the thirst of all visitors was overflowing. Houses, grey and white pebbledash, were dotted along the road with telegraph wires suspended from their roofs making a stop off point for seagulls. Once a fishing community where boats caught mackerel and men weaved nets, it was now a glorious playground of sand and scenery.

The smell of freshly cooked fish and chips in the air started to gnaw at my stomach. I could see a large queue already building up outside the shop so I decided to join it. If I ate now I wouldn't need anything until the following day and there would be no need to set foot in my Grandmother's kitchen. As I drew nearer, I could see a poster in the window, the steam from the fat fryer had made the corners curl and ripple. It was a missing poster of my Mother; the photo had faded taking away her beautiful features, making it difficult even for me to recognise her. Despite my Father's pleas to Chief Inspector Spalding to provide people with more posters, they had come to no avail; Government cut-backs dictated how the police valued my Mother's disappearance. I despised the man for his meticulous ways concerning his accounts, money came before my Mother always.

Pulling my cap further down my face, I joined the queue; no one turned or looked at me as I slowly moved my way towards the counter. The young woman smiled as she served me, telling me how she had been rushed off her feet and not had chance for a lunch break. I wanted to ask her if she had another poster for the window, but thought it might trigger a question. I had passed yet another test of not being recognised, so I quickly left with my food and kept silent. The bench next to the sea wall would be my place to sit and eat, it also hid me from the curious eyes of those enjoying the beach. With my head bent down, I hurried over and sat; my mouth filled with saliva as I unwrapped the chip paper.

A few minutes past and I realised I wasn't alone, children had a certain smell to them which I had always found distasteful; this one reeked of sunblock and from the corner of my eye I could see he was making his way towards me. I took a rough guess at how many summers he had seen. I thought about seven, but my ability to gauge ages had been my downfall. My Mother had remarked many times about how I spoke to everyone as if they were adults, even if they could barely walk. She tried to explain to me that small children may not understand my direct conversation, after that I decided children were pointless, in future I would only speak to those that did not require bending down to.

What was the point in talking to someone who had only just learnt the alphabet?

His short, spiky ginger hair and red face matched his cheeks giving him the appearance of a walking fireball. Unfortunately for him, the ice cream he was devouring didn't seem to be cooling down the furnace between his ears. Most of it was dripping down his chin landing on his red and white T-shirt. He shuffled towards the bench, oblivious of the mess that was falling onto his plastic beach shoes. I carried on eating thoughtfully, my eyes now only focussed on the food before me.

"You're famous," his squeaky voice piped up.

I ignored him and hoped he was talking to someone else, perhaps another person was standing against the sea wall and out of my view.

"Hey, I'm talking to you!" With that I felt the tug of my arm from a small sticky hand, he was now sat next to me. I could feel his eyes boring into the side of my head with the smell of sunblock killing my appetite. Turning my head slowly, I gave him a look that would send most children running. He now had a finger foraging about up one nostril. The look of disappointment was obvious when it emerged with nothing on it, this was another reason for disliking children.

"It is you isn't it?"

I knew he wasn't going away without an answer.

"Listen here, you disgusting little boy, I don't know you, so go away and leave me in peace."

Furious that my space had been invaded I turned my back to him, the stains on his clothes filled me with revulsion.

"You're the girl off the television, aren't you?"

The urge to smack him hard across the face or throw hot chips at him became overwhelming; counting to ten, I slowly turned back to face him.

"I've never been on the TV, so why don't you go find another obnoxious brat to play with."

He never flinched.

"My mom said you killed your mom, did you?"

His head was now tilted to one side and his curious eyes were trying to unpick my thoughts. I couldn't contain my anger any longer and I stood up; grabbing the hot greasy paper I hurled the contents at him. Deep-fried potatoes clung to his ice-cream splattered belly causing the seagulls to descend like lightening, fighting furiously for the food that lay on him and on the ground.

"Your mother should have taught you some manners, you vile little boy."

The combination of seagulls and children was my worst nightmare, so I made my way down to the slipway; once on the beach I could merge in with the crowds and disappear from view. My feet had barely touched the sand when I heard him cry out, screaming with panic for his mother, muffling the squawking birds who were gorging on battered fish.

"Mommy. That girl's hurt me!" his sobs and screams merged into one.

I looked over my shoulder to see his small arms flailing, desperate to frighten off the birds that were now pecking at his clothes.

Serves him right. I hope they mistake his eyes for part of my lunch.

It wasn't long before a woman appeared from the cafe a few yards from where he stood. She gazed about, holding her hands above her eyes to shadow the sun's glare. She was looking for the predator that had made her son squeal. Like a mother hen protecting her chick, she hurried towards him, her arms stretched out to hold him tight.

"Ben, what's happened, my little angel?"

Little angel! Urrggh! He is more like a devil.

The young boy, whom I presumed was Ben, buried his head in her chest, his ice-cream stained face disappeared into the cotton folds of her dress. Occasionally he emerged, gasping for air, then continued to sob back in the arms of his mother, the closeness of her grasp stifling any words he was trying to say. She caught me staring at this farcical sight. Clenching her teeth, she moved towards me, bringing her clinging son with her.

"Did you do this? Come here at once."

Ben made one final lunge for air, pointing his shaky finger directly at me.

"That's the girl you're always talking about, she... she... tried to... to.... hurt meeee!"

Hurt? You don't know the meaning of the word!

I wouldn't allow myself to get tangled up in an exchange of words with a woman who had brought a son up with no manners. Ignoring her demands I carried on down the slipway, soon I would be hidden by the sea wall merging with overweight fathers trying to outdo each other with their sandcastle skills. His cries soon became distant as my walking boots sank into the warm sands. Shells crunched underneath my feet and I weaved in and out of deck chairs. The sea was coming in, already small waves were wetting forts and moats that had been so lovingly sculptured. My mind went back to when I was here with my Grandfather, he would try and build the biggest castle before the foam took it away to a distant shore.

Perhaps my Mother had been washed up on a silent beach, where no-one walked and the sky was empty of birds, unlike this one which was alive with noise. Cormorants and gulls weaved in and out of each other, never touching wings they soared into the cloudless sky. One gull descended and landed directly in front of me; each step I took towards the incoming sea prompted it to follow. My feet were now submerged in an inch of water. Logic told me that they all looked the same, but I was convinced this was the one from my Grandmother's house. He was somehow different, not interested in anything around him apart from my every movement.

To the right of the beach rose a large cliff, high and rugged it towered over the miles of outstretched sand. High waves had begun to crash against its jutting rocks, sending sea spray back to where it came from. Standing on the edge was a figure, I couldn't make out if it was a man or a woman, they seemed transfixed with the violent action of the sea below. I saw the figure turn towards me and wave, a cold chill ran down my spine. The sea seemed to turn a blood red before my eyes and I blinked hard trying to focus on any features. Rubbing my eyes, I waited a few moments before looking back up, the figure had now gone and warmth returned to my body as quickly as it had left me.

I felt a vibration in my pocket and quickly pulled out my mobile, on this golden beach I somehow seemed to have gained a signal. It was a text from Lizzie:

"Hi Matty, hope you're ok, tried to call, but will try again later."

My spirits lightened at the thought I was no longer cut off from my normal world, even if only for brief moments it reminded me I had a life away from here. The time showed 2:07pm, the comfort it gave me filled my heart with hope. Praying desperately that she would answer, I dialled her number; the rings seemed to go on forever and her voice never came.

Damn it! She's probably with that spotty boy and switched her phone off.

My text reply was brief and to the point:

"Can only seem to get signal on beach, will try and ring on landline at 6.30pm."

It was then I noticed I had a series of missed calls, the number said '*unknown*'. No doubt some local Welsh journalist had found out I was here and grovelled to someone in Fleet Street for my number. He'd probably offered to sell his soul to them to get a story, dreaming he would end up working for a mainstream newspaper and breaking the news on the biggest scandal in history.

The gull was still stood beside me, its yellow feet were now submerged in water. It pecked and tugged furiously at my shoe laces, hell bent on gaining my attention. The heat of the sun beat down on my pale skin, I could feel my arms starting to prickle and burn. Kicking out and cursing its presence, he briefly backed away only to return moments later.

"Stupid bird!"

I yelled and jumped with both feet, sending water all over him. He lifted his head and let out a piercing squawk, taking flight and finally leaving me alone.

The beach dwellers were too occupied by playing ball or basking in the sun to notice me or the gull. Their eyes were too busy on the incoming tide, soon they would gather up their hungry children and take them back to caravan city. I had succeeded in getting rid of the two pests now, but the price of this last victory was heavily soaked walking boots. I decided to risk making my way back towards the benches.

Forty-five minutes in this heat should see them dry.

Ben and his mother had now gone and there were no remains of any scraps from my half-eaten lunch. All the benches were now spoken for. No heads turned or words whispered about the girl on the television, the one who never cried about her mother and perhaps was keeping a secret.

CHAPTER 9

Charlie had been right about the interview room; her accuracy impressed me, it was small with light blue walls that had seen many a criminal. The only thing she had missed was the rings on the table left from hot coffee cups, guilty shaking hands had let them spill onto the cheap plywood. I forgave her over the dead bluebottle in the left-hand corner, it could have died after she told me what to expect here. She described the stench of bleach on the lino floor, mopped by the cleaner who only worked nights. Chief Inspector Spalding's eyes were firmly fixed on me, he was sat on one side of the table, his finger poised on a tape recorder.

Why in this digital age didn't the police use DVD recorders? I guess it comes down to money.

Charlie was sitting in the right-hand corner, well away from me. She looked tired, dark circles hung below her eyes, her shirt was creased and the tips of her collar turned upwards instead of down. I wondered if she had been out the night before, overslept and rushed to get into the station. This was the first time I had seen her look a mess and I would tell her afterwards. Father was sat next to me wearing his best suit, beautifully tailored and normally only coming out of the wardrobe if he was due in court. He hadn't been to work since she went missing a week ago. My heart longed for him never to go back and stay with me forever.

A video recorder sat poised on a tripod, its lens pointing and ready to capture my every word and reaction.

Had the police not realised by now I was always the same?

Spalding hit the record button; I couldn't keep my eyes from the port wine stain on the left hand side of his cheek. I wondered if he had been bullied as a child, singled out for being different: if he had, then he would realise what it felt like to be different. I looked down to his bitten nails, even the skin either side of this thumbs had be gnawed away, no doubt from many a difficult case possibly a murder.

"The time is precisely 9:57am, August 4th, 2014. Present with me is," he paused and glanced towards Charlie.

"PC Charlotte Drayton." She looked over to me and smiled.

He then looked towards my Father, prompting him to speak.

"Stuart James," his voice was so quiet it was barely audible.

"Could you speak up a bit, Mr. James?" Spalding sounded irritated, the port wine stain twitched.

"Stuart James," he leant forward into the recorder, almost shouting his name.

"Also present is…" This time he looked directly at me.

"Martha James, and the time is precisely 9:58 and not 9:57." I pushed my phone across the table, the screen showing quite visibly that he had made a mistake.

Spalding's face reddened to blend in with the mark on his cheek, he had never met me before and I could tell he was going to be hard work.

"What time do you make it?" He snapped, turning towards Charlie.

"It's 9:59, sir," she said looking at her wrist.

He took his watch off and shook it, "Cheap rubbish, I knew it was too good to be true."

"I find phones far more reliable. Hadn't we better start again?" I asked.

"Thank you, Martha, for your precision, let's try again." We then went through the same ritual as before, but now he glanced at my phone and gave the correct time.

"Now, Martha, can you tell us a little bit more about the photos you saw in your Mother's study?" His Welsh accent was harsher than my Mother's, he'd probably never left Wales before today.

"I've already gone through this with PC Mayer, there is nothing else to tell you."

"Well, we have a slight problem here, Martha, as we cannot find any record of this so-called project she was working on." He began picking at what was left of his nails, leaving fragments on the table.

"But I saw the pictures." I could tell by the expression on his face he thought I was lying.

"You mention a boathouse. Did she give any indication where this could have been, Martha?" Spalding flicked the remnants of his nails on to the floor.

"That's disgusting!" Filled with revulsion at his inappropriate habits, I got up and looked at my Father, "I want to go home."

"Come on, Matty, calm down and answer the officer's questions. The more he knows, then the easier it will be to find her." He gestured for me to sit down again.

"How come she never showed you the photos, I thought you told each other everything?" An expression of betrayal came over him and he turned his eyes away from me.

Spalding coughed to clear his throat, "Your Father's right, we are just trying to get as much information as possible that will help us find out where your Mother is, come and sit back down. Please?"

I slowly walked back to the chair, inspecting the table to make sure there were no body particles left and sat down.

"We've searched your Mother's computer and contacted all those who had recently enquired about commissioning her, there was no mention of a boathouse."

"So you think I am lying, well I am not, I saw those photographs and the sketches on the wall. She said it was a 'he' that had commissioned her to do it; she was excited as this was totally different to her other work and she was taking a risk."

Spalding looked oddly at me, "A risk?"

"Yes, this was totally different to her normal style."

I then described in detail about 'that' Sunday afternoon how she had shown me her sketches, the photos she'd taken out of the draw that were alive with colour and no lilac was to be seen.

"Did you have access to your Mother's computer, Martha?" Spalding glanced round at Charlie, giving her a wry smile.

"No I didn't."

Father grabbed my hand and tightly squeezed it, "It's ok, Matty, your Mom wouldn't have minded if you did."

"But I didn't, you know I never lie," I said, dismayed at his words.

Spalding said coldly, "We found some software on your Mother's PC, she recently brought it before she went missing." He glanced back at Charlie and nodded.

Rising from her chair she walked over to me; holding out two sheets of paper she said, "Have a look at these. Is there anything on there you recognise?"

The first paper showed a collection of furnishings, from sofas to Persian rugs, lamps and paintings, each one had a tick box next to it. Spalding watched me intently as I studied each image.

"With this software you can create lifelike designs without leaving your front door, very clever if you ask me."

I silently argued with him, he knew nothing about my Mother and how she worked. My eyes then fell to the second page, a large fireplace stood out from all the other pieces. It was that glorious deep red, exactly the same as the one she had shown me.

"This," I said pointing to the image, "it was in the photographs."

Confused and angry I pushed the papers back to Spalding, she had cheated using electronic gadgetry to fool me; but why? My heart sank.

He inspected his newly-bitten nails before saying, "It's amazing what you can do on computers nowadays. I think she may have told you about this new software and you had a go? You said it was nothing like her previous work, so maybe it was your work?"

"Err, I never…" I stammered.

"You're not sure are you, Martha?" He took the paper away from me and handed them back to Charlie; the corner of his mouth slipped into a smirk.

"Were you trying to impress your Mother and show her how talented you could be. Your Father has already told us how much you enjoy art."

I stared numbly at him, watching a trickle of perspiration run down his forehead. My throat began to feel dry, the heat in the room warmed up the bleach floor and I felt nauseous.

"I would like a drink, please."

Spalding grinned, his crooked teeth reminiscent of a dental graveyard.

"Of course. Officer Drayton would you be so kind as to get Martha a drink please?"

"Certainly sir. Is orange squash ok?" The smile she gave me was meant to be comforting to counteract the falseness of her superior, she was trying to make me feel better.

I sat very still, glaring back across the table at a man I thought was an idiot.

"I don't drink squash, it's full of additives and gives you cancer, water will do."

He shuffled nervously in his seat, my face willed him to turn to stone.

"PC Drayton has left the room."

Ah, so the man did have a brain.

"That's very observant of you." I said rolling my eyes.

"We have to note it down for the record, Martha."

"Well, for the record, I'd like to ask why I'm here and why you're not out there looking for my Mother?"

Father's face flushed red, I'd seen that uncomfortable look many times when he'd been to parents' evening.

Charlie soon appeared carrying a plastic cup of water; she handed it to me then resumed her place back in the corner.

"PC Drayton has entered the room."

I placed the cup precisely over one of the rings on the table, I'd counted eighteen, but now there was one less to irritate me.

"You didn't answer my question?"

"At this moment in time we have officers scouring the area where she went missing. It's vital that we investigate all leads, Miss James, if you can think of anything else that may help us with our enquiries then please let us know."

My hand confidently picked up the cup, not shaking or spilling a drop, I downed the water in one.

"I've got nothing else to say."

He looked frustrated with me, something was gnawing at him and I knew what it was. I imagined myself sitting in his seat staring at a young girl who'd just lost her Mother. Where were the red puffy eyes, the distraught expressions and the ringing of hands? My mind quickly travelled back to its own body.

"Interview terminated... time... err..." He shook his watch again then took my phone off the table.

"Time, 10:14am."

CHAPTER 10

It took me an half an hour to walk back. I stopped occasionally along the way, the heaviness of my sodden boots making the hill harder to climb. Every now and then I checked my phone for a signal, but all the screen displayed was '*no service*'. The elderly lady who I had previously seen leaning on the gate was now gone, the road was empty and still, even the cricket had become silent, its vocal chords parched from the heat. I embraced the solitude, the road was mine alone to amble along, but soon it would come to an end and I would turn into that drive. I desperately hoped she had gone out or even better had disappeared into an abyss like my Mother. I contemplated turning back, but my thighs ached and my puny knees trembled at the thought of being forced to descend the hill again. Why had I forged so many letters in my Mother's handwriting, excusing me from all physical activities at school? I hated exposing my body on a hockey field or in a gymnasium and never envisaged myself wanting to have muscle power that would drive me forward in the Welsh countryside.

I made the last few steps onto the gravel, the squawk of a seagull welcomed me back. It was perched high on the roof, golden eyes fixed on my every movement. She was there, not in the previous smart outfit I had seen her in before, but now in linen khaki shorts and a t-shirt. Her hands were deep in the soil below the windows, the white nets above her showing off sparkling clean windows. A white transit van was parked up, painted on its side were the letters "*Harper and Son, Landscape Gardening - no job too small.*" I took a deep breath in before approaching her. As I drew nearer it struck me how old she looked. All traces of makeup had been removed, the deep lines above her lips now visible. The gravel gave me away, she looked up, the previous hostile expression had gone.

"Oh thank goodness you are back, I have been so worried."

"I would have been out longer, but it was too hot."

"Yes, it is a real scorcher today, I am really sorry about earlier, it's just that... err... I am findings things difficult."

"Well, that makes two of us then!"

I kicked at the gravel, sending it flying towards the van, startling the bird on the roof also and making it take flight.

"Who's here?" I asked, pointing towards the van.

"Ah, that's Peter. I called him after you left as you made me think about how much I had let the garden go after your Grandfather died. It's too big a job for the likes of me, so Peter's out the back having a look to see what needs doing. I thought if he cut the lawn maybe you would like to sit outside and paint. Is that ok with you, Martha?"

I noted a hint of sarcasm in her voice. She slowly stood up, arching her back, her muddied hands resting on her hips and let out a groan.

"I have also asked him to look at your bedroom window."

"Fine," I muttered.

This change of heart gave me a feeling of uneasiness and I wondered why she was being so accommodating, she also hadn't asked me where I had been! Was she not slightly intrigued that I may have been spotted or said something inappropriate to one of the locals. Brushing past her, I made my way to the garden gate; someone was whistling loudly and extremely out of tune.

A tall young man stood with his back to me, knee deep in the grass. I could see he was carrying a clipboard and pen. He was wearing a short-sleeved white t-shirt, wrinkled and in desperate need of an iron. The back pocket of his jeans was torn, exposing glimpses of maroon pants. He never heard me approach, his eyes were too busy fixed on the old tree at the end of the garden.

"So, you must be Peter." My voice startled him and he dropped the clipboard deep into the grass.

"Jesus, you made me jump." He turned towards me his perfectly formed white teeth flashed with a grin. The colour of people's teeth had always held great importance to me; I had got cleaning my own down to a fine art. I found that my ritual of brushing them for precisely 5 minutes and 45 seconds was sufficient to keeping them perfect. Any more seconds would cause my gums to bleed, the stained spit in the bowl would make me feel sick. I made a mental note to ask him how many minutes he spent brushing. His sandy brown hair was cropped close to his scalp, pale blue eyes twinkled as he put out his hand to shake mine. Touching strangers was not a habit I enjoyed, so I quickly placed both by hands in my jean pockets.

"You must be Martha," he stated. Realising I wasn't about to acknowledge his gesture, he lowered his arm and with sleight of hand, retrieved his clipboard from the grass.

"There's a heck of a lot of work to do around here. Dad said it probably wouldn't take long to get sorted, but he sure was wrong."

"I did offer to cut the lawn for her, but Grandmother wouldn't let me."

"Well, I'm not surprised, that rusty old lawnmower looks as if it should be in a museum."

I gave him a reluctant nod.

"I can't believe she has let you set foot in the place, make sure she pays you upfront before you do any work."

Peter let out a roar of laughter, exposing his gums; he'd been brushing for far too long.

"I take it you don't like her, huh?"

"I hardly know her, I have only met her a few times. Anyway are you any good at fixing bikes? I can pay you?"

"Well that depends on what sort of bike it is, I'm no good at fixing Suzukis."

So he was a joker, one of those people who struggled to take anything seriously. I needed to be more precise if our conversation was going to continue.

"This is a pedal bike; as far as I can see it's all working apart from two flat tyres and maybe a bit of oil on the gears."

"Ah the old one in the shed." I didn't think it was possible for his grin to get any wider without consuming his ears.

"It belonged to my Mother and I want to use it."

"Well I can take a look to see if there's a pump lying around, but first I need to crack on and get this quote done. That tree needs to come down for a start, it looks bloody dangerous to me."

Using his pen, he pointed towards the large tree. It had only been a few hours since my fingers had caressed the bark, but the hours had somehow changed to years, ageing it beyond recognition. The trunk looked weary, leaning heavily to one side, many of the branches had now broken off as if a high wind had ravaged it in some terrible storm.

"It wasn't like that yesterday," I said, confused as to why it had dramatically changed.

"It must have been like that for some time, we get bad weather here in the winter and no doubt the poor old thing has had enough." I shrugged my shoulders, what did I know about trees.

"I'll leave you to it, then; let me know if you can fix the tyres."

"Will do."

"By the way your jeans are ripped."

He looked bemused as I turned and walked back to the house, the kitchen door was wide open and I was in need of a drink.

She was there, sitting silently at the small table writing on a notepad.

"I'm making a list of things that need doing around the place," she said without looking up. "Why don't you make your Grandmother a nice cup of tea?" Her wry smile unnerved me, making my hands tremble.

Even though her eyes never seemed to leave the table, I felt as if she was watching me as I backed away towards the kitchen sink. Each step I took seemed to match the rhythmic tapping of her soiled fingernails.

"I was wondering if you wanted to go out for supper this evening? I stupidly didn't get much shopping in, it's been awhile since I've had guests." She placed the pencil down finally looking across to where I was standing.

"Well... I... errrr... I... I did try and have something earlier, but...," I stopped, deciding to keep the earlier encounter with that boy to myself.

"I thought we could take a trip into Laugharne, a new bistro has opened up and I haven't tried it yet."

What on earth was going on? My mind whirred at the thought of her going out and socialising. Apart from her trips into Tenby for essentials, she seemingly never left the four walls of this house. Father had told me many times of her paranoia about being spotted somewhere and part of me understood why. However, I was still hungry, and if this was the only way food would enter my mouth, then so be it.

"Whatever you want to do Grandma." She didn't seem phased by the delay in my response.

"Good, that's sorted then, after you've made my tea you can go and freshen up." Her false smile was almost grotesque.

Stirring the tea bag around the mug, I watched the water turn to a muddy brown, the milk separated and curdled as it rose to the top. Placing it down in front of her, she hesitated and sniffed the contents of the mug before taking a large gulp.

"I think the milk maybe off."

"Nonsense girl, I've always preferred things a little sour."

After dabbing her lips with the edge of the table cloth, she slowly closed her eyes and began to rock backwards and forwards. Deep within her throat she began to drone, the same monotonous note over and over again, quickening as her throat constricted more. The muscles either side of her neck bulged like large rubber bands. Another discordant sound joined in, single squawks in the form of an ornithological morse code. A gull was approaching the house, finally perching on the window box behind her. I watched as her face began to contort and twist whilst the beak of the bird violently thrashed against the glass. I feared it would shatter and so would she; for a brief moment I thought she had suffered a stroke.

"Grandma, are you ok?"

I studied her hard, looking for any signs of paralysis on one side. I became more fearful when I realised she wasn't physically sick; my head began to spin with the realisation her illness was of the mind.

She opened her mouth taking in a large gulp of air, her eyes were now wide open.

"I'm fine dear, you go and get yourself ready."

I knew the heat of my bedroom would be unbearable, but it seemed more welcoming than watching an elderly lady's mind torture herself. Alzheimer's was unknown in my family, but I'd read it could deal a cruel blow to anyone. Leaving her to resume swaying, I quickly made my way out of the kitchen into the hallway.

"I'm looking forward to spending time with you," she called after me.

I made my way upstairs, imagining the gull flying behind me, its grey wings spread out across the staircase, swooping and confusing my lank black strands for lugworms. The door to my bedroom was wide open. I raced in slamming it shut behind me. No phantom birds would be allowed in here. The stifling heat hit immediately, choking me with invisible hands. The window was still stuck solid as if someone had fixed the frame to the sill with an everlasting glue. As I looked through the glass, I could see Peter leaning over the bike. The vision of seeing another human brought me back to all sense of normality. I prayed he was repairing the tyres, freedom and fresh air was what I needed.

Soon after, the cool water from the shower tumbled down my sunburnt arms, no longer white and ghost-like; my skin was scorched red, stinging from the Pendine sun. I thought about the boy I had met and realised I'd been lucky that he was the only person who had recognised me. Mother had told me how different Laugharne was, how the people embraced everyone who entered the village, even the unusual. She said they were beautiful, along with the view of the estuary. She had spent many days there as a young girl, along with her friend Sara, they would share secrets and teenage years.

I patted myself dry with a towel made of sandpaper, as it was the only one I had been allocated, I then used it to wrap my long black dripping hair into a turban. Washing it had always been a chore, so I decided that tomorrow I would cut it off and leave the remnants in the bedroom, hiding it for someone to find and ponder whose scalp it belonged to.

Thankfully, Lizzie had packed my one and only dress. Stepping into the sleeveless black cotton I caught the reflection of myself in the bedroom mirror, it was one I didn't recognise; stood before me was a woman. My stick-like figure looked more curved, the beginnings of freckles peppered my nose and my eyes seemed less dark. I'd bought the dress in case they'd ever found a body, it was fitting for a funeral, but thankfully it had stayed unworn. Tonight I would wear it, apart from being cool it was the only thing suitable for dining out. By the time displayed on my phone it had taken me a good hour to get ready, sixty-two minutes had transformed me into a fresh-faced looking girl whose stomach was gurgling with hunger. After slipping my feet into plain black pumps, I made my way back down the stairs. Peter's voice could be heard from the kitchen, but as soon as I entered his words stopped, his eyes scanned my body and I wished I'd chosen jeans and a T-shirt. Grandmother had transformed herself back to perfection, each grey strand neatly swept back and secured by a black velvet bow. Her crisp white blouse had been neatly tucked into a blue pleated skirt. I stood there nervously fidgeting with my hair while she looked me up and down. When she realised I was wearing black pumps, a glint of disapproval came across her face.

"Your bike's fixed," he said.

"Yes, Peter's been kind enough to fix it for you, he's a good boy." She turned her head towards him.

"Thank you," I said. "I can ride out tomorrow and take my sketchbook."

"No problem. Right then, Dylis, I'll be back early in the morning I think the lawn's the first on the list, we can't have you sneezing and coughing, Martha," he said grinning. His smile had a familiarity about it and for one moment I thought somewhere in the past our paths had crossed.

"Could you see if you can get my bedroom window to open before you go? It's stifling up there."

"Sorted, I checked it first thing when I arrived."

Usually I could tell a liar, their expressions gave them away from the first instance. Eyes would flit to one side, hand movements showed awkwardness and their feet would shuffle. Peter looked at me direct, his body still and there was no hint of any deceit.

"I tell you it's shut solid. I've tried it again and it won't budge."

"Martha, don't be so rude. If you'd been here earlier you would have seen him fix it instead of going off God knows where," she said with an indignant look.

"It's ok, I'll take another look, but I think you need to start eating more spinach to build up those muscles of yours." His laughter filled the kitchen cutting through the awkwardness between her and I.

Who was he to tell me what to eat, I thought as I followed him upstairs to my bedroom.

"Blimey, it's bloody hot in here," he said as he stepped in my room.

He walked over to the window and placed his hands either side of the frame, with one push it slid up letting in a flood of fresh air, filling my lungs with an early evening summer breeze.

"I don't understand it..." My words faltered.

"No worries, it's open now and I'd best get off." And with that he left.

I stared out of the window and could now see the garden in its entirety. The old tree seemed less bent, as if someone had propped it up and was supporting its brittle branches. Leaning against it was my Mother's bike, the sun was shining down on the red metal frame. He must have cleaned it, I thought, it looked as if it had hardly been used. The low rumble of Peter's van could be heard making its way off the drive and down the hill, I was now alone with her and my thoughts. Something quickly caught my eye, a large shadow appeared across the left hand side of the long grass. At first I thought a child had let go of a kite that had been carried by the sea breeze up to the house. Leaning further out of the window to see what could be creating such a shape, I was greeted by a mewing sound. Large broad wings of cream and brown spread out into a shallow V shape, its fan-like tail quivered as it remained suspended in mid air. This bird of prey was searching the garden, its golden eyes scouring every inch looking for a small mammal. I was transfixed by the power of this flying beast as it started to circle above the tree. It let out another mew before flying over the high beech hedge into an area I had never noticed before. This old house was neighbour to a meadow of wild flowers, jostling with each other for space in a blaze of colours, an ideal hiding place for mice and rabbits. My heart sank as it swooped down, some poor animal was about to die, grasped by talons that would soon carry it away to a nest of death. The knocking on my bedroom door stopped me from seeing the victim, another bird of prey had arrived. This one wore silver bangles and was calling me.

"Martha come down quick, your Father's on the phone."

CHAPTER 11

The hallway now smelt of polish, a welcoming reminder of the fragrance from home, tourist leaflets next to the receiver stood neatly in a pile. She'd been busy while I had been getting myself ready.

"Hi Matty, can't talk for long. I've landed in Singapore and I just wanted to check you're ok."

The clarity of his voice took me aback, considering he was thousands of miles away.

"I'm ok, how was your flight?"

He then proceeded to tell me that the food on the plane was awful and how much he was missing me.

"As soon as I get to Melbourne I will call you, angel."

"Ok" was all I could utter. What I really wanted to say was, 'No, you've left me here with a woman who's stark raving mad' but of course I didn't because she was standing behind me listening to my every word.

"So, what have you been up to?" He paused. "I hope you have been staying out of trouble."

"Not much, we're going out shortly to Laugharne for supper."

"Well, well, well, how have you managed to persuade her to go out?" He sniggered.

"I'd best go," I sharply replied. Conscious of her presence.

Placing the receiver back in its cradle I turned towards her and noticed the fresh application of lipstick.

"Right, are you ready? We'd best set off before it gets too busy."

She clearly wasn't going to ask about my Father.

Laugharne was a short distance away, 5.6 miles to be precise. Mother had told me many times how she had ridden her bike to see Sara, each time trying to break her own personal record by knocking seconds off her journey. "Pendine may be known for its land speed records, but I was known locally as the fastest girl on two wheels." She would laughingly say. I was a novice on a bike, but perhaps by the time Father came back I could beat her time.

My Grandmother's car was a rusty old Mini, neglected and in desperate need of a clean. As we travelled down the road towards Laugharne, the sounds of gunshots ricocheted in the distance. The Ministry of Defence owned the land to the right of us and people were forbidden to enter. A large wire fence stood high against the road and I occasionally caught a glimpse of an army vehicle that stood poised ready for practice manoeuvres.

She was humming all the way, her eyes fixed on the road, not once glancing round to take in the scenery. Her silver bracelets occasionally brushed against the steering wheel, adding percussion to the notes that were coming from her mouth. We passed the caravan park on the left, all neatly lined and facing towards the sea. Children were playing outside, making friends with each other, no doubt sharing stories of where they came from.

Mother had told me the first view of the estuary was one of God's paintings. I had no idea who God was and never understood why people worshiped a being that was so cruel. If he had painted such a sight then there must be some menace in his strokes. As we descended down the hill into Laugharne, I hoped I would not be disappointed. Grandmother seemed oblivious to the on-coming car that was blaring its horn, the driver gesticulating at her for being too far over his side. She slowed up as we entered the town and pulled into the car park in front of the estuary. The water swept in circles, leaving exposed mud flats. Sand dippers pecked at its richness, while a heron glided above them in the hope that some fish had been left by his brothers. The castle towered over the water, like a king ruling all that flowed beneath it. Its dark walls stained by history were now home for rooks and jackdaws sitting silently amongst the stone crevices. Inlets were carved deep into the marshland and a small boat was moored amongst the rushes.

Perhaps there was a god after all, as the sight before me was breath-taking. I hadn't noticed my Grandmother get out of the car, it was only when I heard the 'tap tap' on the window that I realised I was on my own.

"Come on Martha, we won't get a table if you hang about."

I could see the impatient look on her face return. Her eyes darted around, examining the area for visitors who might recognise us.

Stepping out of the car, I followed her across the road. Her steps were swift and purposeful, she had no time for pausing or looking back. A large stone cross stood in the middle of the square, either side of it were small shops and two pubs facing each other. People were sat outside on benches, drinking ale and lighting up cigarettes.

"This is a pretty village" I called to her.

"Don't you dare call this a village, Martha, it's a township and the people are very proud of it," she said spinning on her heels, her face full of anger.

After my verbal slap across the face I proceeded to follow her to the doorway of the bistro, above its entrance was a sign "The Owl of Laugharne". The two windows either side were lit with an array of Tiffany lamps, brightly coloured leaded glass giving the windows a welcoming glow. At the base of each lamp was a sculpture of an owl, all in different poses of flight.

More damn birds, but at least these ones were handmade.

It was a small restaurant with tables dotted about lit by candles in red rose glasses. The smell of pasta and freshly-baked bread filled the air and hunger pains reminded me I'd hardly eaten anything all day. All the tables were full, people noisily chattering over glasses of wine; thankfully, no one looked up as we searched for an empty table. A young girl came over, her large brown eyes and smile welcomed us, she pointed over to a small table in the corner. Two plaits hung down over her shoulders, her face doll-like and beautiful. Grandmother gave her a smile that I'd not seen her give before, warm and genuine.

"Thank you Gwyneth."

"How lovely to see you Dylis, Mom said you might pop in." Her voice was light, almost tuneful.

Grandmother pulled out a chair and beckoned me to sit opposite her. I wondered how my long gangly legs would fit under such a small table and, as I squeezed myself in the candle tipped slightly before blowing itself out. Gwyneth produced a box of matches from the pocket of her apron, turning her smile towards me. She left us alone to examine the menu. I held it high enough to block out my Grandmother's stare, and playing safe, decided to have pizza. Placing the menu back on the table, my eyes turned to the shelves on each wall. From large intricately carved tawnies to small porcelain barn owls, each shelf bowed under the weight of what seemed like a 'Museum of Owls'. I couldn't help, but think she would be well suited sat amongst them, her eyes sharp and piercing, her small pointy nose that had the uncanny resemblance of a beak.

Oh how I wished I could laugh.

"Well, this is nice." Her one eye squinted at the menu, no doubt her vanity prevented her from wearing glasses.

"What is? The bistro?"

She was up to something, no doubt poising herself to fire questions at me.

"Us being out together. I was thinking while you were in Pendine, we don't really know each other, do we?"

How did she know I'd been to Pendine?

"I suppose not," I replied. My voice was hesitant, the urge to get up and escape was overwhelming.

"I was always too busy with the Guest House to get to know you, Martha, however, your Mother would often tell me how well you were getting on at school."

This was a lie, Mother said she never asked about me and would return from Wales furious at the lack of compassion given to her own daughter's child.

"So, how are you coping since your Mother went?" There were no tears in her eyes, it was if she was talking about a stranger.

"I have Dad and I'm coping fine." It was now my turn to ask questions. "How are you coping, after all she *was* your daughter?"

She blanked me.

"So?" My words came out much louder than intended, rising above the chattering behind me.

"It's not *was* Martha, she *is* my daughter. I believe she's still alive, don't you?" She leant over the table, grabbing my hand tightly.

Her words took me aback, I had always thought that she was convinced Mother was dead and my Father or I were to blame. As the days and weeks passed since her disappearance my thoughts changed hourly, my brain had become a pendulum swinging from one thought to another. One minute I would imagine her walking through the front door then, seconds later, I expected the police to call to say a body had been found.

"She was like you once, then things changed." Now she was whispering, her face only a few inches away from mine.

"What would you like to eat?" She let go of my hand to pick up the menu once more, this time moving it backwards and forwards trying desperately to focus on its contents in the candlelight.

How could this be? Mother had always been so different to me. She could laugh when I couldn't and shed tears of which I had no understanding.

"Martha, is that you?"

I glanced up to see a woman standing next to us. I guessed she was in her late forties, much taller than myself, her brown cropped hair framing a pale boyish looking face. It took me awhile to realise who she was, I'd been about ten the last time we'd met.

"Hi Sara, yes it's . . . . ." Before I had chance to finish she bent down, flinging her arms around my neck.

"Oh my, look how you've grown. Your Father never told me you were coming." Her voice became cold as she turned her head towards my Grandmother. "Hello Dylis."

"It was arranged at short notice." Droplets of saliva jettisoned their way towards me as she spat the words out, I felt sick.

"Well how lovely to see you. How long are you here for?" Sara cast a wounded look back at me.

"Just two weeks, Dad had to go away on business."

"We must catch up properly, Matty, I have to shoot as I'm on call." Moving closer to my ear she whispered softly, "You've got my number, I'm off work all next week."

"Martha's going to help me around the house so you won't be seeing much of her."

Her words fell on deaf ears as Sara was already walking away, leaving me curious as to how she had heard her whispers. I didn't know Sara well, on the few occasions I'd stayed in Pendine she rarely visited. She lived in Laugharne, but her veterinary job was based in Swansea. My Mother always went to see her alone, in fear I may come into contact with fur and have a serious asthma attack. She had two dogs and they were her life, any spare time she had would be spent walking the estuary. Apart from my Mother, she only enjoyed the company of animals. I never understood this, but I concluded that animals and I weren't meant to be.

"So, before we were rudely interrupted, what would you like to eat?"

I looked blankly at her.

"Pizza, please."

She called Gwyneth over, ordering a pasta dish for herself and my pizza, which I insisted on being simple. My appetite soon left me as I wiped my mouth in fear of the remnants of her saliva still being there. It wasn't long before the food arrived and her lipstick soon became smudged with olive oil and basil.

"Never liked that woman." A single strand of spaghetti hung from her mouth, the owl image came flooding back as I imagined it was a remnant of some poor mouse's tail.

"Never married you know, it's not normal," she said, sucking it up in one go.

"Perhaps she's never found the right person, and it's rude to talk with your mouth full."

That soon shut her up.

She resumed eating, this time occasionally dabbing her mouth with a napkin; I ate my pizza in silence. When our plates were finally empty, she asked for the bill, I offered to pay my half, but she proceeded to tell me how nice it was to spoil her only Grandchild. Leaving the exact money, and without a tip she got up from the table and walked towards the door. Embarrassed by her thriftiness I rummaged through my purse, handing over a five pound note to Gwyneth, who seemed surprised by my gesture.

"Thank you," she said. "I hope you don't mind me asking, but are you Martha?"

"Yes. Why?"

"So glad to have met you, do come again." She smiled, walking away and ignoring my question.

No doubt she had seen my face from endless newspapers, but her smile hopefully meant she hadn't taken in the rubbish that had been written about me. When I stepped outside my Grandmother was nowhere to be seen. I walked over the road to where more people had gathered outside the pubs. A man staggered towards me, his glass spilling beer over the cobbled floor and his face red with too much ale.

"Merch bert," he said, bowing and holding his glass high in the air.

I took a step back, fearing his unsteady hands would spill beer all over my dress. He repeated his words, this time bellowing them out for all to hear. His Welsh words made no sense and, in fear of being publicly accused of something I quickly made my way to the car park. My Grandmother was sat inside the car, her eyes tightly closed and the engine running. Fearing she had fallen asleep and giving me no escape from drunken words, I banged hard on the passenger window. Finally she stirred, opening her eyes and unlocking the door, enabling me to climb in and slam the door tightly. I glanced in the wing mirror, making sure we hadn't got company.

Water now engulfed the mud plains, the estuary had now become a sea. Gulls and cormorants dived into the deep water, fighting each other for food that was alive. The small boat that had been hidden by rushes now floated, showing off its blue main hull.

"You took your time," she said, putting the car into reverse.

"I decided to leave a tip."

"I'm going out tomorrow, not sure what time I'll be back," she said. "I'll leave a key for you in the hall, don't forget Peter's coming early in the morning."

Was everyone around me ignoring my words or only answering the things they wanted to hear? Damn it! Those precious hours I would have alone would now be interrupted by a man wanting cups of tea and talking about the price of grass turf.

The journey back was as slow as the one going, her humming resumed like a discordant hymn.

"What's that tune?" I asked, but she didn't reply.

I expected a certain seagull to fly above the car and follow us back, tuning in to her sounds. Our journey home showed only signs of pigeons, lazily dawdling in the middle of the road to peck at crumbs discarded from car windows. Grandmother took care to avoid them, her concentration on the road ahead made the journey more pleasurable. She fell into deep silence as we approached the house, the sound of the tyres against the gravel drowned out by the familiar squawking on the roof.

"I'm going to get changed and have a rest. I'll see you before you go to bed."

I watched with bemusement as she walked down the hallway towards a door under the stairs. Turning the handle quickly, she disappeared closing the door behind her.

Surely this couldn't be her bedroom. It had previously housed the old boiler that fed the central heating pipes to all the rooms; as far as I was aware there was no bedroom in its dark cellar.

It wasn't fitting as a room to sleep in, unless she enjoyed resting with decaying pipe work and spiders. Tiptoeing towards the door, I dared myself to follow; the handle felt icy cold, sending a shiver down my spine. I recoiled, hoping my sharp intake of breath hadn't been heard. The swinging pendulum of the Grandfather clock simultaneously came to an abrupt halt. If it hadn't been for the chill that was running through me, I would have found the silence of this old timekeeper a relief. I slowly stepped back towards it, recalling childhood memories of the metal hands that could choke a young girl. Opening the case, I gently touched the pendulum, sending it sideways; it soon resumed its sway and the familiar threatening clunk started up again. I almost felt it groan with relief as it went back to its mechanical life. I also breathed a sigh. I may not have liked the sound, but it gave me a sense of normality in this old house. Checking the time on my phone to make sure it corresponded with the old clock, I wondered how many minutes I would have before she reappeared. The evening light would soon be fading and darkness would fall upon the house once more. Before the last shadows were cast I decided to venture back into the garden and inspect my Mother's bike. The key was sitting in the lock of the kitchen door waiting for me to turn it.

Summer's warmth had left Pendine for the night, the air was now cooling quickly. The long grass swayed slightly as I waded towards the bike, which stood propped up against the tree. Peter had adjusted the saddle; no longer the height for my petite Mother, my long legs now touched the pedals comfortably. I balanced myself with one hand against the tree, the other on the handlebar. It was then I noticed a difference in the grass, a small path had been flattened, leading from the base of the trunk to the hedge it led out towards the meadow. Peter must have gone over to check the hedges, disturbing the grass as he walked. This path, however, was too narrow for human feet, it also appeared to have been downtrodden over a period of time, exposing soil instead of grass.

I thought no more of it and looked up towards the house, my eyes following the windows until finally they rested on my bedroom. The window was shut, rage billowed up inside me. She'd obviously sneaked back upstairs to close it, determined to suffocate me over the coming days. Enough of her little games, I would go back inside, find her and words of truth would spew from my mouth. The next morning I would get the first train home. I had enough money to get a cab to Tenby as well as my train ticket back to Birmingham.

All angry thoughts soon came to a halt with the sound of a gunshot; a loud boom shot across the meadow next to me. My hands slipped away from the handle and tree that were keeping me upright. As I tumbled towards the ground the smell of sulphur filled the air, a warm trickle flowed down my brow bringing darkness to my eyes.

CHAPTER 12

I could tell by the softness of her skin she had returned, small petite fingers slowly caressed my black hair: the way only a mother can soothe a brow.

"Martha, open your eyes."

No more bad dreams or broken hearts, my eyes would open to see her comforting me.

"You've had a fall and bumped your head, please wake up."

My head throbbed, something warm was trickling down my forehead. I slowly raised my hand, liquid oozed between my fingers.

"Have I been shot?" I murmured.

"No, you've just had a nasty fall off that damn bike. I knew I should have thrown it away."

The voice was no longer soft, silver jangled around my face as the hand turned bony and cold. Slowly, I opened one eye, the pain above it caused me to wince. The other eye followed, its lid briefly stuck together with something sticky.

"It's getting late, try and stand up."

For a few seconds my vision blurred, but soon the shape of her extended hands became all too clear. I grasped them, heaving my torso to a sitting position. Barefooted and clothed in only a dressing gown, she took my full weight with both arms, heaving with all her might to get me to stand. I noticed the haze of the moon above her head, silver that slipped into blue. Nausea came deep within my stomach making its way upwards until the remaining undigested pizza tumbled onto the grass.

"We need to get you in the house and clean that wound up, hopefully it won't need stitches."

Putting one arm around my waist, she tugged to move me

forward. My legs trembled as they tried to steady themselves, if I fell again I would take her with me. Her head turned back quickly, nervously scouring the garden she then quickened her steps, almost dragging me to the back door. I sensed her fear as she took one final look before slamming the kitchen door behind us. She led me along the hallway to her back room, I caught a glimpse of myself as we passed one of the mirrors, my face was ashen.

Fumbling for the light switch, it eventually clicked, turning on a small chandelier, its crystal droppers had long gone. A million candles could not illuminate this room, it would always be dark and cold, even if the heavy curtains allowed themselves to be pulled back.

"Why don't you open the curtains, it's so dark in here you can barely see a thing?"

"I like it like that," she whispered, as she nudged me towards what seemed the only chair in the room; it was hers.

The floor was strewn with newspaper cuttings about my Mother, every Fleet Street rag that had covered her story now acted as a carpet.

"I feel safe here." She looked around as if someone else was in the room, a sense of unease was in her eyes.

"What are you scared of?" I asked, bending to pick up a paper with the headline "*Meredith had no enemies*".

"I'll go and get the first aid box." Ignoring me yet again, she walked towards the door.

The room felt stagnant, old and yearning for someone to bring it back to life. Using the arms of the wing-backed chair, I lifted myself up; the pain in my head returned with a vengeance, but I was determined to let light in. The heavy velvet was unforgiving, but with both hands I yanked each one back. The moon's light outshone the chandelier, floor boards creaked under my feet as if sighing with relief that there was another human in the house.

Now that extra light had entered I could see more of what was in the room. A writing desk stood along one wall, letters were stacked up, tied with string on its leather fold-out table. Next to it sat a large silver tray with an empty decanter, once full of sherry that Grandfather would secretly sip after a long day. In one corner, a spinning wheel lay on its side, yarn hung from it, moth-eaten, never to be turned into something beautiful. The fireplace was the central focus of the room, made of cast iron inlayed with hand-painted tiles, it housed a fire basket. No coal or burning embers were to be seen. A few inches above it hung a mahogany mirror, heavily carved with exotic birds. Wings outstretched the frame, intertwining with one another, making a graceful sea of feathers. Reflected in the mirror was a glass case, inside were hooks holding keys of all shapes and sizes. My heart began to race in the hope these were the keys to open the doors below my bedroom. The jewellery on her wrists was my warning sign, giving me enough time to make my way back to the chair.

She was holding a first aid box, opened ready to nurse my wounded head. As her eyes darted from me to the open curtains she let out a gasp, the box slid from her fingers spilling its contents to the floor.

"What the hell have you done?" she screamed.

She would punish me for this, I knew it.

I recoiled as I watched her race over to the window; blindly, she thrashed at the velvet until finally each met the other. Frustration hit out, the anger inside me mounting. I kicked the empty first aid box towards her.

"It needs more light in here, you won't be able to see my head. What are you afraid of, one minute you're happy to go out, then the next you hide away? None of this makes any sense."

Rage overwhelmed any pity for her.

"I'm not afraid," she snapped. "This is my house and I'll do as I wish."

I thought about my options as she stood before me, wild and tormented. It wasn't compassion that prevented me from retaliating, but the thundering pain above my eye. She took a deep breath in and, as she exhaled, I prepared myself for another torrent of fury, instead the red mist in her eyes disappeared.

"I need to clean that wound up before it gets infected."

Picking up a sealed wipe, she gestured for me to sit down. I bit my lip as she wiped the congealed blood from my brow, the antiseptic seeped deep into my cut, making me wince once more.

"I heard a gunshot, that's why I fell off my bike," I said, briefly pushing her hand away from my head.

She shrugged.

"Who owns the land next door?"

"I don't know his name, he bought it a couple of years back, before your Grandfather died. He often shoots rabbits, next time I see him I will ask him not to get so close to the hedge."

"He could have killed me, is it him you're scared of?"

"God, no." A hint of a smile started to appear. "I hardly ever see him, he's some property developer from London who only comes here occasionally."

"Did Mom know him?"

"No, she never met him. What are you trying to suggest, Martha, that he accidentally shot your Mother thinking she was a rabbit?" She let out a laugh, but there was nothing remotely funny about my thoughts.

She could be lying dead in the field now, covered with only wild flowers and honey bees who sipped from the nectar of death. I knew Pendine had been searched thoroughly, heat-seeking helicopters had flown over all the area. Residents had come out in their droves meeting at the sea front cafe before dispersing with maps provided by Inspector Spalding.

"I think Charlie should be told about him, they may have missed something."

"Call her if you wish, but I know what her answer will be, don't you think I've thought about every possibility. They even took cadaver dogs on the land next door, but came up with nothing." Her tone seemed genuine.

"What did you mean earlier at the restaurant when you said Mother used to be like me?" I hoped her kinder side was emerging, giving me answers.

"Soon you will understand and all will become clear. How's your head feeling now?" she asked, holding my chin gently.

I understood nothing, the comparisons between my Mother and I seemed ridiculous, my Grandmother's mind had truly gone.

The pain in my head was beginning to ease, my stomach felt less nauseous, but every sinew in my body felt drained with tiredness. I wondered what time it was, my hands fumbled in the stitched inside pocket of my dress, searching for my loyal friend.

"My phone, it's gone! It must have dropped out of my pocket. I need to go and look for it." Desperation and panic hit me. I bolted out of the chair towards the doorway. Her small frame moved like lightening, blocking my exit.

"It's too dark out there, you won't find it in all that long grass, take a look tomorrow when Peter's here."

"But I need it." My voice was desperate.

"Why do you need it, Martha, if you want to call anyone then you can use the phone in the hall?"

"I want to know the time." I tried to get past her, but she pushed herself harder against the door.

"It's late, look for it tomorrow, when you feel a bit better."

"I feel fine." I shouted, my face was now so close to hers I could feel the powder brushing against my cheek.

I didn't feel fine, adrenalin rushed through me bringing back dizziness. I put out my arm to steady myself against her.

"You need to get some rest, Martha, I won't go out tomorrow if you're not well. You may have concussion and I have to keep an eye on you."

This was the last thing I wanted to hear, I took my arm away, mustering up all the strength I had to stay upright.

"No, you go out, I will be ok. I'll go to my room and rest on the bed."

"I think that's for the best, you go on up now."

She stepped away from the door to let me pass. I managed to convincingly walk without losing my balance. Hanging on to the stair rail, I slowly climbed each step. I could feel her watching me from the bottom, waiting for me to trip or fall. When I reached the landing to turn to the second flight, I looked back; she was nowhere to be seen, but her humming could be heard. As soon as I entered my room I unzipped my dress, letting it fall down my legs, not caring to hang it up it I pushed it to one side with my feet. The window was still firmly closed, but I'd gone past caring. The old brass bed embraced my naked body as I fell backwards into its coiled mattress, the pillowcase felt rough against the skin of my cheek.

Sleep came quickly only to haunt me with a dream. I was walking along a corridor of doors; occasionally I would stop to peer through the lock and the eye of a bird would stare back, the stench of death impregnating the wood.

I awoke with a startle, high pitched screams were coming from outside, but these were not human noises. I quickly got out of bed, gathering the patchwork quilt to cover my body I made my way to the window. Pressing my face against the glass I tried to focus on what could have made such a chilling sound. As my eyes became more accustomed to the dark I could see a small light near the tree, it appeared to be flashing on and off, then pausing for a few seconds before restarting.

It was the light from my phone.

Minutes passed, there was only silence. Convincing myself that the noise was a part of my nightmare, I grabbed my jeans and jumper and got dressed. Carefully, I crept downstairs. Every now and then a step would creak. I paused and waited, expecting her to call up and demand I go back to bed. The only sound I heard was my heartbeat thundering with excitement. I made my way down to the bottom undisturbed and, hopeful my phone would soon be in my grasp, I darted into the kitchen. The key turned easily. I stood for a while, listening out for the cellar door to open before stepping out into the blackness. The grass was wet under my feet as I made my way to the outline of the tree. As I got to its base, I heard a rustle from the hedge next to the meadow. It startled me for a second. *Rabbits,* I thought.

A green light suddenly shone in front of me, I bent down, my fingers digging deep in the grass to pick up the illuminating screen. Wiping it with the sleeve of my jumper I gasped, I had a signal!

I counted the number of steps I'd taken away from the tree, five had given me my lifeline back. One step back and the signal died. Returning to the exact position, I scrolled down the menu to see who had tried to contact me. It was then I began to shake, the phone nearly slipping through my fingers back into the grass.

The name of the caller was displayed… It was my Mother!

Steadying my hand, I pressed the return call button; placing the phone against my ear, I waited as it rang.

"The person you are trying to reach is currently unavailable, please leave a message or try again later."

"Mom, it's Matty." If there was one time I wanted tears to appear it was now. "Please Mom, it's Matty, tell me where you are, we've been so worried. I'm staying at Grandma's and…"

There was a click, my time had run out on the answer phone. I stared at the screen, she was alive, I knew it.

Suddenly something rushed by, brushing my jeans before disappearing into the hedge, it felt too large to be a rabbit. Within seconds I began to sneeze and my eyes had that all too familiar gritty feeling. I knew it was only matter of time before my chest would tighten, so I made my way as quickly as I could back to the house. By the time I reached my bedroom I was gasping. I fumbled for my inhaler that was lying on the dressing table. The first burst had no impact. I pressed again praying for the second blast to work. Slowly, my lungs began to relax, my throat loosened enabling me to take a deep breath in.

Lying back on my bed, I tucked the phone under my pillow, grateful for the day which had given me hope.

I will find you, I promise.

CHAPTER 13

"I wanted to make sure you were ok before I went." She was outside the door, her bracelets reminding me I wasn't at home.

"I'm feeling much better you go, I'll be fine," I mumbled.

As soon as I heard her step away from the door, I slipped my hand under the pillow, feeling for my phone to make sure last night wasn't a dream. Returning back to Birmingham was now no longer an option, I could even tolerate my Grandmother's behaviour for a few days if this meant the end of a nightmare. My fingers traced the large bump on my forehead, it felt sore to touch, but my mind was full of hope.

Half an hour passed. I wanted to make double sure she'd gone. Grabbing a T-shirt and jeans from the wardrobe, I quickly got washed and dressed. I hadn't time to count the brush strokes against my teeth or worry that my hair looked greasy, I needed to investigate the house before she returned. I made my way downstairs, listening out all the time for her voice. Today was not the day for having conversations with old women who chanted at birds.

The front door key had been left on the hall table. I placed it in my pocket and pulled out Charlie's card. It was Saturday and, as I dialled her number, I prayed she would be on duty. She often worked weekends, grateful for the extra shifts as money was tight.

I waited.

"PC Charlotte Drayton, how can I help?"

"Charlie. It's me Martha… Martha James."

"Oh, hi Matty, how are you doing?"

My words tumbled out, telling her I was in Wales, and last night my Mother had tried to call. She attempted to interrupt, but I gave her no chance.

"There's a meadow next to the house, I heard a gunshot, Charlie. You need to find out who owns the land…" I continued.

"Woah! Slow down a bit, Matty. What did your Mother say?"

"Nothing, I didn't get to the phone in time, it was her number though." I could feel my neck turning red with frustration. There was a stony silence. "Charlie, you there?"

"Yes, Matty, I'm just jotting things down."

"The gun, someone's got a gun. They may be holding her as a prisoner."

I tried to imagine her on the other end of the line, her smile disappearing, as she knew I never lied.

"Lots of people own guns, Martha, especially in rural areas, I'll check out who owns the land and see if they've got a licence."

"I want you to send someone round now, I've got proof on my phone, it's my Mother's number."

"You know we spent weeks trying to trace your Mother's phone, unless someone removed the SIM card we would have found it by now."

She was being rational as always. The redness of my neck now rose into my cheeks, I would burst with temper.

"Then perhaps they did. Send someone now!"

"I'll have a word with Inspector Spalding and get back to you, is that ok?"

It was obvious by her tone that my Mother's case was no longer top of her list. She'd moved on or her private life had become more exciting.

"Promise me you'll speak to Spalding."

She knew exactly what I was getting at, she believed in God and told me numerous times that you shouldn't promise something you can't fulfil. I once asked her if she would burn in hell if she broke a promise, but a smile was her only reply.

"I promise. How's your Gran?"

I wanted to believe her.

"Thank you," I said, knowing that in her mind Satan would be waiting for her if she didn't make that call to Spalding.

"She's not well."

"Oh, I'm sorry to hear that Matty."

"It's ok."

"Has she heard from your Mother?"

It was my time to be silent, had she heard from her and not told me?

"I don't know, she's behaving really oddly."

"In what way?"

Now she seemed more interested in the behaviour of my Grandmother than the possibility my Mother was alive.

"I've got to go, call me on her landline if you hear anything."

I felt alienated from her, so much time had passed since she held my hand; I gave her no chance to say goodbye and hung up.

Someone was near, the sound of shuffling gave them away.

"Your Gran said it would be ok for me to make myself a drink whenever I wanted."

I turned to see Peter standing in the kitchen doorway, his face was serious, showing no sign of those perfect white teeth.

"How long have you been there?" I needed to know what he'd heard.

"I've only just come in, I've been in the garden for a good hour, I'm surprised you didn't hear the noise of the lawnmower." There was a hint of a smile.

"Ok." I studied his feet to see if they were doing the '*lying dance*', and for a second I thought I saw one foot shuffle awkwardly. "You best carry on then," I said blankly.

I waited until he turned to go back into the kitchen then made my way to her sitting room. As soon as I entered, it felt like winter. The remains of the first aid box still lay on the floor. The latch securing the box on the wall slid up smoothly. I took the keys from their hooks and placed them in my pockets. I made my way to the first floor; one by one I tried each key until finally I heard a click. I cautiously stepped in, expecting the stench of death from my dream to hit me.

The first guest room was as I remembered, simple and tidy, the beds made up with plain white linen. A sweet smell hung in the air, lavender bags were neatly placed in each corner of the room. I glanced around in relief that there was no sign of death. Then I saw it. I quickly recoiled back to the doorway, I was no longer alone, his emerald eyes motionless and still. I trembled in anticipation that the outspread wings would envelop me. Minutes passed and neither of us moved. I shuffled hesitantly towards the cormorant sat poised on the bedside cabinet. I heaved a sigh of relief. The cormorant was long dead, frozen in time by chemicals to preserve his dark ominous form. Hesitantly, I stroked his body, burnished brass feathers sculptured in a quilt of magnificence. This poor creature who once soared the skies was now a prisoner in this decaying house. Opening up empty drawers and wardrobes, I inspected every inch of the room, keeping one eye on the bird in case he came to life.

After finding nothing apart from a discarded comb, I closed the door behind me, locking it and returning the key back to my pocket. I struck lucky with the room opposite and unlocked the door on my first attempt. The same smell filled my nostrils, sweet lavender giving off a pungent heady perfume. This time a barn owl stared out towards the window, cream and brown feathers woven into each other, its face outlined with a heart-shaped mask. No longer alive to hunt and dine on mice that scuttled through Welsh corn, no more a predator. Again the room was empty of any belongings or traces of life.

Each room that followed housed a different bird, from bullfinches to blackbirds then, finally, a heron. Its long legs stood proud and tall on a wooden plinth placed in the middle of the room. The beak had been forced open and pointed towards one of the lavender bags that had disintegrated with age. I visualised it waking from its deadly sleep, pecking at the dried flowers in desperation for food. Sadness filled me as I remembered the heron soaring across the estuary of Laugharne, wondering if this poor creature had ever dived into those waters. As I closed the door on the final room I looked at the last two remaining keys, one was larger than any of those I had used, the other small, more fitting for a cupboard or wardrobe. I remembered the cellar door and hoped this larger key would provide answers as to why my Grandmother rested there.

As I made my way downstairs I could hear Peter in the hallway, he was not alone. I drew still, eavesdropping on a voice I did not recognise.

"Thank you, I would appreciate that." The voice sounded elderly.

The large key slipped from my fingers and clattered down the last remaining stairs. I cursed myself for being so clumsy.

"Martha, I was just coming to look for you, this is Police Constable Matthews, he said he needed to speak to you?"

"Yes, thank you." An awkward silence fell between us, Peter looked puzzled, I could tell he was longing to ask me why.

"Right then, I'll leave you to it." He turned to go back into the garden, then shouted, "You ok, do you want me to stay?"

"I'm absolutely fine, thank you."

I couldn't tell if he was just being curious or damned nosey, either way I wanted him to leave us alone.

"You'd best come through." I gestured towards the kitchen.

The lawnmower started up, it was now safe to speak. "How come you got here so quickly?"

"I received a call from Inspector Spalding, I gather you have some information you wish to pass on?"

"You never answered my question."

"I was passing the area anyway. May I sit down?"

Unapologetically I pulled out a kitchen chair, his knees clicked as he slowly lowered himself down, he looked tired and in need of a holiday.

"You look too old to be a policeman."

"I am, not long before I retire." He smiled, unfazed.

This explained his lack of hair and paper-thin skin that just about covered the bones on his skull, the lines either side of his cloudy blue eyes were deep.

"I take it you already know who I am?" I asked sharply, taking my customary position when being interviewed by the police.

"Yes, Miss James and I'm sorry for your loss."

"I have no loss, she's alive!"

He nodded, "I gather you had a call?"

Pulling my phone from my pocket, I thrust it towards his face. "Here take my phone and look, she tried to ring me."

He moved back slightly in his chair, maybe he feared I might strike him.

"I can't see a thing, Martha."

"What?" I turned the screen back towards me, the battery had completely died. "Wait here."

I raced out of the kitchen, thundering up the stairs until I arrived at my room. Its normal place was beside my bed, plugged in ready to give life back to my timepiece. I scoured every inch, pulling clothes from the wardrobe and shaking them in desperation. The gap under the bed was too small for it to hide, it was nowhere.

The kitchen was empty by the time I returned. I was just about to shout his name when I heard laughter and his face appeared at the backdoor, in his hand was a mug of hot tea.

"He was good enough to make me a drink."

What in God's name was Peter thinking, entertaining complete strangers?

Matthews tilted his head to one side, "You don't mind, do you?"

"Not at all, why not invite the whole bloody force round, I'll get some biscuits in!"

Matthews gave a wry smile as he sat back down at the table.

"Did you find your charger?"

"No, but you must have the facilities to charge it?"

"Ok, Miss James. I'll take it back to the station to see what we can do."

Giving him a look that said '*I will kill you if you lose this*' I handed over my phone. As he walked towards the door I noticed him limping.

"When do you retire?" I asked.

"Next week, thank God. I am booked in to have the old knee done in a month's time. Anyway, Martha, I'd best get off." He slapped his leg and let out a sigh. I was struck by his resemblance to some bumbling detective I'd seen on TV, who'd always ended up solving the crime, much to the bemusement of everyone around him.

I showed him to the front door, but he paused before stepping outside.

"I understand you're staying with your Grandmother, is she around?" His eyes darted back down the dark hallway.

"No, she's gone out and I'd rather her not know that I've spoken to you."

"Why's that?" His tone turned inquisitive.

"Err… she's not well at the moment, she's gone to the doctors." I think this may have been the first time I'd ever lied and I prayed my body language didn't give me away.

"Well I think it might be wise you have a word with her, I can pop back later before I finish if you want?"

"That won't be necessary; I'll see how she is when she returns. I don't want to give her false hopes at the moment." I kept my arms rigid beside me, trying with all my might to stop them from twitching or rubbing my face.

"That's a nasty bump you've got on your head."

"I fell off my bike, it looks worse than it is."

Oh for God's sake just go.

"Right then, fingers crossed we come up with something."
I waited until he got in his car; he drove off slowly and only looked back once to wave. The sound of the mower could still be heard, thankfully Peter was still working and not eavesdropping on our conversation. Stepping out onto the gravel drive I gazed up towards the roof, there was no seagull watching me. As I went back into the house I wondered which room the wretched bird would end up in. My bedroom was the only one left without an example of taxidermy. I would wring its miserable neck first and dump it in the sea before it had chance to join the others. The cloudless sky was bird-less; apart from the sound of grass being cut the house was still.

The large key was still on the stairs. I quickly picked it up and made my way to the cellar. The lock resisted my attempts, not wanting me to know what was behind it. A chill of apprehension ran through me as I grabbed the key with both hands and twisted it violently.

Click.

The pull chord switch was above my head. The light flickered before finally casting a dull glow on the stone steps. My hands brushed against the cold dank walls as I descended, visions of flesh-eating zombies flashed before my eyes. I'd seen far too many films where cellars held creatures of the night, hiding in shadows and lusting for blood. There were no such fictitious demons here, it was just a normal dank cellar that smelt musty with mould mixed with the heavy perfume she wore.

The boiler was fixed to one wall, its pipes like spaghetti weaved their way up through to the ceiling. A wooden bench lay against one wall, scattered with medicine bottles, makeup and nail varnish, a small mirror leant precariously on its edge. On the other side was a single bed, its sheets thrown back in a crumpled heap. At the foot of its base stood a clothes rail, her dresses and suits hung from the metal pole, a variety of shoes stacked underneath it. My pitiful deranged Grandmother was sleeping here, the khaki shorts and T-shirt I'd seen her wear yesterday hung over the headboard.

Picking up one of the medicine bottles from the bench I instantly recognised the name on the label; it had been given to my Father a week after Mother went missing. *'Just a little something to help you sleep,'* the doctor had told him. He only took them for a day, vomiting and headaches followed, so he flushed them down the toilet and vowed not to take another one. Another bottle had the word *Lithium* on it. I knew it was a chemical of some sort, but had no idea what it was used for. As I stepped back my foot caught something, a large wooden box was jutting out from underneath the bench. I bent down to pick it up, common sense told me she could return at any moment and I was meddling with time, but I was no longer feeling 'sensible'. After last night's call from my Mother, playing dangerous was the only option, adrenalin urged me to take a look.

The lid fell open, spilling piles of photographs across the cellar floor, a sea of faces I didn't recognise, many standing outside the house ready to depart home. Grandfather enjoyed this small pleasure of taking snapshots; so many came and went he liked to capture their final moments. I began to gather up the photos when I noticed one particular shot of a young teenage girl cradling a baby; next to her stood an older woman who I presumed was the mother by the way she was looking down at the child. The girl looked blankly out towards the camera, uncomfortable and awkward with what she held. Studying her face, I soon began to realise this was my Grandmother as a young girl; she looked barely fourteen, youth, however, could not disguise that stern look. Placing them all back in the box, I spied one final photo, the vibrancy of its colours came as a refreshing change to the monochrome dullness of the others. Kneeling under a tree was a young girl, her flock of auburn curls cascaded down her blue and white check dress. She was pointing at something out of the camera's view, pale and serious she mirrored my daily expression. It wasn't the recognition of her emerald eyes or beauty that caused my hands to tremble, it was the branches of flowers above her head. The tree no longer old and dying was bursting with youth, it was perfect, it was lilac.

CHAPTER 14

She would have known nothing, apart from the photo of a child surrounded by a blaze of her favourite colour, all was put back in place. Keys now returned to the cupboard on the wall, the box carefully placed under the bench, I was meticulous. The picture of my Mother was hidden in my suitcase, slipped into the rip of the lining, it now belonged to me. What made her change from a stern child into the carefree woman we all knew? Grandmother's words now rang true, maybe she was once like me? What stared back at me was a child who appeared starved of all emotion, who longed to be shown how to smile.

Silence. The Lawn Mower had come to a halt.

I gazed out of the kitchen window wondering when the seagull would return; my hands would be ready to throttle it. The sound of a chainsaw broke my thoughts. By the time I stepped out into the garden, a large branch lay butchered on the neatly mown grass, sap trickled from its centre like old tears.

"Stop!" I screamed.

His headphones drowned out my plea; oblivious to my presence, he raised the saw ready to cut another branch. Not thinking about the consequences of my actions, I raced up behind him, kicking him hard in the back of his leg. The chainsaw fell from his hands, spinning and whirring across the lawn ready to slice anything in its path. He stood there for a few moments, panic-stricken, waiting for it to come to rest. I watched as he hurled the headphones to the ground then walked over to the machine to turn it off; he caught sight of my guilty look.

"For Christ's sake, you could have killed me!"

"You can't cut the tree down, it's still alive, look." I pointed to the sap oozing from the felled branch, wanting to magically glue it back where it belonged.

"I don't give a damn about the tree, don't you realise how dangerous those things are?" His face was red with rage.

"Sorry." I tried my best to sound convincing.

"I should bloody well think so, no wonder you've got bumps on your head if you go round acting as reckless as that."

"Please don't cut anymore, there must be a way of saving it?" I opened my eyes as wide as they could go.

"Hmm."

"Please." I begged, blinking rapidly. Lizzie told me this was called fluttering in order to get your own way.

It worked hook, line and sinker.

"I must admit I thought it was well and truly dead, but that branch still has growth in it." He walked over to where it lay and rubbed the sap between his fingers. "Yep, you're right, perhaps with a prune it may recover."

"Thank you. How's your leg?" Showing concern might possibly avoid him telling my Grandmother.

"A bit sore, but I'll live, you've got a hell of a kick." Now a smile returned, I let out a sigh of relief.

"What time is it?" I asked.

"It's time for some lunch. I've got some sandwiches in the van, fancy one?"

I nodded. I hadn't thought about food all morning, I'd evaded the dry sawdust and milk in order to check the rooms.

"Good, I'll go and get them."

I studied him as he walked away and tried to form an impression in my head. My experiences with the opposite sex were few and mainly coloured by their stupidity. He seemed innocuous, his body language showed no signs of threats towards me.

Positioning myself under the tree, I stretched out my index finger and pointed; calculating the size of my Mother's frame against mine, I pondered what she'd seen. All that came into view was the small pathway I'd seen the night before. Now the lawn had been cut the indentation had become more exposed, bare earth ran in a line from where I sat to the base of the tree.

"It's rude to point." He was trying to be humorous.

He sat down next to me and offered me a sandwich from his already open lunch box. I peeled back the bread, double checking the cheese had no mould.

"How come the grass hasn't grown there?" I asked, still pointing with my other hand.

"Animal." His words were barely audible from the large bite he had taken.

"What sort of animal?"

He paused, swallowing hard. "Probably a cat, they like to follow the same track."

"Do you know who owns the field next door?"

"Of course I do, it belongs to my Dad, why?"

"Your Dad!" I exclaimed; my astonished look took him aback.

"Yep, you seem surprised." He took a final bite.

"Grandma said it belonged to a property developer from London."

"Well that's partly true, we did live in London for a while when I was younger and he does own quite a lot of land around here. He keeps saying he will build on it one day, maybe a house for when he retires."

I paused, gathering my thoughts.

"How long has he known my Grandmother?"

"I gather he's known her for a few years, occasionally helping your Grandfather with the garden, but I do most of the work now. So, why are you interested eh?"

Grandmother was spinning yet another lie, she knew this man much more than she was letting on.

"I heard a noise last night, a gunshot that threw me off balance, that's how I fell off the bike."

"Ah, I see, he's partial to a rabbit stew." His laugh would be infectious to most.

"I don't see what's so funny," I said, pointing to the bump on my head.

Peter took a moment to consider.

"I'm sorry it frightened you." The familiarity of his smile hit home again.

"Have we met before?" I asked.

He was now studying me; beginning with my feet his eyes scanned my body finally looking up into mine.

"Nope, can't say we have. I hope you don't mind me saying, but you're a lot different to most girls I've met."

"What do you mean?" I snapped.

"Well… err… I don't know how to put this… but you're very direct."

A look of embarrassment swept across his face, he turned his eyes away.

"I see little point in talking to people unless I need information from them."

He flinched, visibly wounded by my words.

"Is that why you're talking to me?"

This was true, but I held back from telling him so.

"So you've not seen my photograph in the newspapers?"

"I don't read that rubbish, in fact I don't read much at all apart from gardening books. Talking of which, how come this tree's so important to you?"

I don't know why, perhaps it was because he'd taken note and changed his ripped jeans or forgiven me for kicking him, but something compelled me to tell him about my Mother. He sat silent, listening intently as I told him about her love for the colour lilac, her disappearance and my reason for being here. I kept secret the phone call; that information was for the police alone.

"This tree means something, it was obviously important to her." I looked up at its branches and dead flowers, longing for them to spring back to life and bloom.

"Is that why the police came to see you?"

I nodded.

"I'm sorry to hear you've had such a rough time, but what am I going to tell your Grandmother, she thinks the tree's coming down?" He began to look worried.

"Tell her the truth, that it's not dead and pruning it will save her some money?"

"Well it will, cutting the whole thing down would be a costly job, she's a bit of an odd one." The smile on this Welsh boy's face returned and it gave me comfort. Above our heads clouds were forming into giant pillows, twisting and turning, soon they would block out the afternoon summer sun.

"I think we may have some rain, you'd best carry on."

"I'll chop that branch up first and put it in the van along with all the grass cuttings."

I watched as he stood up, his steps were forceful and with purpose as he walked away.

He would make a good boyfriend for Lizzie, their laughter blending into one, living happy ever after without a Great Dane in sight.

I returned back to the house to get my sketchbook before resuming my position against the tree. My precision in line drawing was well suited for this giant of white bricks she called a house, each window perfectly square, the distance between them making it easy for me to replicate. I would ignore the climbing ivy, that required a technique I had no skill for. Occasionally, Peter came over to glance at my progress, complimenting me on my eye for exact detail.

As he carried the last part of the branch down the garden to load into his van, I felt droplets of rain against my forehead. Irritated that my pencil lines were now becoming smudged I ripped off the sheet, throwing the crumbled ball across the grass.

"Why have you done that?" he asked, looking bemused.

I shrugged.

As he picked up the chainsaw, I realised soon I would be alone.

"Have you got time for a drink before you go?"

"Sure have, Martha, see you in a min."

A mug of tea had been made for his return, I'd even found some out-of-date biscuits hidden away in a cupboard.

"Can I ask you something?" I said passing him a stale digestive and hoping he couldn't tell.

"Sure, fire away."

"I went to Laugharne yesterday and a man said something to me in Welsh."

"What did he say?"

"He said *merch bert*."

"Well, let me think, my Welsh isn't up to scratch," he said, dipping a biscuit into his tea.

"I think *bert* means girl and *merch*..." He started to snigger.

"*Merch* means what?" I demanded.

"It means pretty, he was saying you were a pretty girl."

"He was drunk and you're spilling your tea all over the table."

My cheeks began to burn, a sensation I had never encountered before.

"I do believe you're blushing, Martha."

"No I'm not," I stammered. He was taking me out of my comfort zone and I now wanted him to go.

"It could have been my Dad, we live near there, he loves his ale, but so do many in Laugharne."

"It's a beautiful place, you're lucky to live there." My face was now ready to burst into flames.

"You'll never go to heaven unless you see Laugharne, very few people leave the place."

"Why's that?" I asked.

"Why would you want to? There's work for people on the outskirts and when they come home they see a landscape that beats anywhere else in the world."

I had to agree. My parents had taken me abroad many times, Mother wanted me to experience sights that had inspired many artists, but, much to her disappointment, even Tuscany had left me numb.

"Did you go to the boathouse?" he asked.

That word soon cooled down my face, I wondered if it could be the one I had seen in her sketches.

"Where is it?"

"Bloody hell, Martha, you can't visit Laugharne without visiting Dylan's boathouse."

"Who's Dylan?" The only Dylan I knew was a folk singer whose songs blasted through our house at home, Father said he was the '*God of Music*'.

"Dylan Thomas, the poet. He lived there for a few years with his wife, his boathouse looks across the estuary."

"Oh, him." This was my second lie. I felt a sense of satisfaction, it was getting easier to deceive.

"Well, I'm going to ride out tomorrow on my bike so I can have a look."

"I can take you if you want, that bike and you don't seem to get along." His smile gnawed at me, I'd seen it so many times, but on whose face? I wondered if this was what people called 'being asked out on a date'.

"No thanks, you'd best go. I'm sure you've got other things to do."

"Ok, but if you change your mind here's my number." He handed me a torn off piece of paper from his notebook.

"Here, take it and tell your Grandmother I'll call her tomorrow about the tree."

Reluctantly, I put the paper in my pocket knowing full well I would never ring it. Chatting and getting information from him was one thing, but socialising and maybe him wanting to kiss me filled me with disgust.

I showed him to the front door, the rain was coming down in torrents and there was no sign of my Grandmother's car. I hadn't a clue where she'd gone or when she would return.

"Please tell me the time," I shouted as he opened his van door.

"Hang on. I have to switch the engine on to see the clock."

I waited until I heard the roar of the motor, he wound his window down and bellowed.

"Four o'clock, see you again, I hope."

He drove off down the driveway and was passed by another van; this one was much larger, more like a delivery truck. As it pulled up, the rain hammering down on its metal roof. I watched as a man got out of the driver's seat, he was holding a slip of paper.

"Delivery for Miss James," he said.

"I haven't ordered anything, you must be mistaken."

"This is the 'White House'?"

"Yes."

"Ah good. I've got the right address, can you sign for this?" He handed me the paper and a pen.

"What is it?"

"Your groceries and I'm getting soaked."

My Grandmother had come to her senses and realised that we couldn't survive on thin air, I signed the slip.

"I'll bring the stuff in then."

I watched as he unloaded overflowing carrier bags and as he passed them to me, I placed them down in the hallway until he handed me the last one.

"I don't think I've delivered here before." Water was now dripping down his cap leaving a puddle on the tiled floor.

"You're making a mess," I snapped.

"I don't think I shall deliver here again." He looked at me sternly.

He'd barely stepped out of the door before I slammed it behind him, infuriated that I had to not only drag each bag through to the kitchen, but also wipe up after him.

I opened up the bags, there was enough food to keep us going for weeks. Fresh meats and vegetables spilled over the floor as I tried to lift them up onto the kitchen worktop. Meticulously, I stacked the food in the fridge and an assortment of cereals in the cupboard. The freezer was packed to the top with a variety of instant meals and, as I finally closed the lid, I heard it.

The scream that had pierced the night had now returned, high pitched shrieks rose to a peak, sending every vein ice cold. It was getting nearer the house, continuously calling. With each step, the coldness spread throughout my body. Was it crying out to me?

The back door was still ajar. I raced over, my heart pounding, any saliva that was in my throat now ran dry, I could not swallow. My hands fumbled for the back door key. Its cries were getting nearer as each second passed. Finally I heard the key turn and lock, I pushed my back against the door, whatever was out there wanted me.

CHAPTER 15

The rain no longer battered the slate roof and all was silent. I waited, my legs struggled to hold up this young girl who did not believe in monsters. If I stayed here long enough my Grandmother would come back, the sound of her car would frighten off whatever was outside. It dawned on me, this '*beast*' which made ungodly sounds could be the reason for her fear and I must be the one to stop it.

I waited.

It would have been easy for me to run up to my bedroom and hide, but I didn't. The past had taught me a lesson, the only thing I truly feared was news of my Mother's death. Now she was alive, I felt defiant. Knowing the kitchen drawers held a variety of knives, I crept across the floor in search of the most lethal weapon I could get my hands on. Grabbing a carving knife, I made my way back. I'd never killed anything before, but Father had once told me of a case where a woman had slit her husband's throat in self-defence. She had suffered years of torment until one day she snapped. If I was to murder, then perhaps he could save me in court, after all I wasn't a '*normal girl*' in the eyes of most. I unlocked the door and slowly peered outside.

The sun was now breaking through the clouds. I stepped out, the knife gripped tightly in my hands. I regretted Peter leaving, even the exchange of a kiss seemed worth his company. I could have washed my lips in the cool pools of rain that had collected on the lawn and no-one would have known. I glanced down the garden, my eyes scouring every inch, I was ready to lunge with the knife.

Instinct told me to look at the tree. I was being watched. A large fox sat at the base of the trunk, upright, his eyes fixed on my every movement. This one bore no resemblance to those I'd seen dead on the road back home, their bodies crushed under the tyres of busy traffic. He was very much alive. His burnt orange coat glistened in the breaking sun, eyes golden as corn narrowed as it saw the knife between my fingers.

Surely this could not be the creature that had caused me to contemplate spilling blood, something else must be out here?

I moved closer, already my eyes were beginning to itch from the thought of his fur being near me. He opened his long brown snout, baring white teeth that had no doubt devoured many a rabbit. For one brief moment I thought he would spring from the grass, running towards me, snapping and snarling at my ankles, sending me fleeing back to the kitchen. This mouth action was only a yawn, his tongue smacked against his lips, finally closing without threat.

"Shoo!" I cried.

I was now a mere foot away, the sight of the knife made no difference, he showed no desire to move. This was the closest I had been to any animal. I waited for my chest to tighten and cursed the fact my inhaler was not in my pocket. Blinking occasionally from the sun's rays, his white breast calmly rose and fell unperturbed by my presence. Words soft and deep rushed through me, bringing back pain to my forehead; these were not sounds uttered by human lips, strong and deliberate they were aimed at me.

"*You are Chosen, YOU are one of the Trinity.*" The sounds rumbled through my brain.

The knife slipped from my hand, nausea returned to the pit of my stomach as I felt the graze above my eye. I shook my head frantically, desperate to clear the voice coming from inside it.

"*YOU have been called, tomorrow when the sun is down, we will see you where the flowers grow.*"

My body tensed and sent more blood flowing to my head. I fought the dizziness determined to stay upright. The madness that was possessing my Grandmother was now taking over me. My eyes began to swell and my vision blur, if I didn't get back to the house I feared I may go blind. The fox drew nearer, it was now stood at my feet. He raised his one paw and rhythmically stroked my leg, I could hear his pulse combine with mine.

"Do not fear what you hear."

He repeated this time and time again. This soothed me into a trance and took my heartbeat to a place it had never been. All pain left me and, as I held out my hand, his ochre coat beckoned me to stroke it. Softness fell between my fingers, each hair felt as if it belonged to me alone. Heat rushed through my body, for the first time in my life I felt alive, invigorated by his beauty.

The fox heard the noise before me, his ears twitched as he nervously backed away.

"Don't go," I whispered, but it was too late.

He turned and I watched as the white-tipped tail disappeared through the hedge, not making a sound or looking back at this girl who longed for him to stay. My eyes had stopped itching, I felt what would become a tear enter one eye.

I was now alone.

The sound that had sent him running was my Grandmother's car, she had returned, along with a gathering of crows that were circling above the house. Twenty or more of these sombre birds swooped down towards the roof, then folded their wings in unison as they settled on the tiles next to the chimney. The clunk of the car door sent them calling, louder than any seagull they were welcoming her back.

My footsteps felt light as I walked back towards the house, something deep within was changing me, a new sensation of discovery. I heard her call for me from the hallway, now her well-groomed grey hair lay loose across her face, the lipstick was gone, her lips bitten in fury. She placed her hands over her eyes, wailing like a real widow should mourn.

"Tell them to go away!" she cried, her head swaying back and forwards uncontrollably.

"Who Grandmother?" I moved closer, I no longer felt anger, but pity.

"The crows, please make them go away." She crumbled to the floor. I leaned down towards her, resting my hands on her shoulders.

"Shh… there's nothing to be afraid of, they are just birds, come into the kitchen and I'll make you a cup of tea."

"They are a MURDER. A murder of CROWS. Did you not learn anything from your Mother." Her sobs were almost choking her words.

Realising that unless they took flight she might fade away before me. I walked out the front door. The crows were still there, lined up as if ready for battle. I grabbed some gravel and threw it as high as I could, sending it bouncing across the roof. One bird spread its wings and took flight, the others carried on calling and took no notice of my presence. This time I threw with such force I toppled backwards, small pieces of gravel embedding themselves into my elbows. I flinched with pain, but determination to make them leave overshadowed any discomfort. A large piece struck one crow, causing it to sway before flying off. The others followed suit, crowing at me with bitterness. I waited for a while making sure each one had gone before re-entering, she was still huddled on the floor, her hands pushed hard against her ears.

"They've gone. It's ok now."

She looked up at me, a lost child who desperately wanted to be held. I put my arms gently underneath her elbows and lifted her light frame until she stood. She buried her head deep into my chest, her body trembled as I stroked her hair.

"There, there, come and let me make you a drink."

I led her into the kitchen, no longer wary of this woman who gave birth to my Mother. I wondered, as she wiped her tears away how long she had left on this earth, her frailty gave me the answer. She sat silently staring into her teacup, the bracelets were no longer on her small pale wrists, large bruises marked her skin where once hung silver.

"You've been hurt." I held her hand, looking at the purple marks that we're getting deeper by the second.

"It's nothing," she said.

"What's happened? Where have you been all this time?"

Tears began to well up again in her eyes; she lowered her head to avoid my gaze.

"You must tell me." I placed my hand under her chin and turned her face upwards. She needed protection from whoever had done this; birds were not capable of inflicting such wounds.

"You have to leave, Martha, it's for your own safety. I shall call your Father and demand he comes back." She struggled against my hand, trying to lower her head again, but I was determined to get to the truth.

"I'm not leaving you here alone." I couldn't believe my own words and how they had changed in a matter of hours. "Tell me who hurt you," I demanded.

"Oh my dear child, I wish I could, but I can't. If only things had been different and I could turn the clock back, I would give anything for you to stay."

"Then let me." I got up and walked towards the hall, no matter how much I disliked Inspector Spalding he needed to know about this.

"Where are you going? Please, I'm begging you, Martha, don't tell anyone." She raced towards me, her eyes wide open, filled with terror. "They won't believe you if they know the truth."

I thought about the words that had entered my head as I stroked the fox, I wondered if people would believe me if I told them I heard voices.

"I'm not in danger anymore." Her voice now calm, she sat back down and sipped her cold tea.

"Tell me about the birds." I expected my words to send her into a rage, but she sat silent, stroking the tea cup. "Why were the crows gathered on the roof?"

"I'm forbidden to tell you, until you become *Chosen*."

That word Chosen again, had I been picked out to be my Grandmother's salvation?

"How will I be CHOSEN and by WHOM?"

"I cannot say, it is out of my hands, but you are on the right path to find out, you are already changing."

This was true, my whole body felt alive with strength and a yearning to cast away anything that belonged to the old Martha.

She came closer, her nostrils wide as she breathed in the air around me until finally her nose rested on my hair.

"What are you doing?" I asked, perplexed.

"Breathing in freedom." she whispered.

"Breathe away." I wanted to humour her and brushed my hand against her cheekbone. She pulled back.

"Oh God. I forgot to get us any food. You must be starving."

"The delivery arrived Grandma, we have tons of things to eat." *Her memory was clearly fading fast.*

"I haven't ordered anything, I don't know what you're talking about."

I showed her the entire contents of the freezer only to be told how grateful she was and how she would reimburse me. I succumbed, convincing her that Father had given me enough money to treat her. She sat and watched me prepare supper. I kept it simple as my culinary expertise was limited, but the omelette should satisfy us both.

As we ate, we exchanged the occasional word about school and my hope to go to Edinburgh. She told me that when she was a young girl she longed to travel, but it had become impossible. I wanted to ask her why, but, as she spoke the sadness returned.

"Did Peter come?" she asked.

I nodded.

"How was he, did he ask where I was?"

"No, he's cut the lawn, but wants to talk to you about the tree."

"Your Mother loved that tree, she would sit for hours sketching underneath it." A hint of my Mother's smile broke through on her face. I rose from my chair, my arms outstretched and begged to hold her, she came without question. We stood in silence, embracing each other like long lost friends. Every minute of this day was throwing new experiences at me, perhaps I would laugh and dance one day.

"You must be tired Grandma, why don't you go and rest?"

"Yes I am, I think a good night's sleep will clear my head. I will be fine by tomorrow so if you want to go out then, don't worry about me."

"Are you sure?" I asked.

"I'm already a prisoner here, you must now learn to spread your wings."

She walked away without looking back. Wondering if this would be the last time I saw her, I followed her to the door under the stairs. She disappeared without giving me the chance to offer her my bed; exchanging places with her seemed a small price to pay for a woman who had little time left. The face of the Grandfather clock looked more mournful than ever, it had had enough of life and no matter how many times I swung the pendulum it always came back to the same resting place.

CHAPTER 16

The murmuration of starlings told me it was dusk, they swooped in a whispering black cloud across the sky, ready to take roost in some old building far away from the house. My bedroom window stayed open with ease, blowing back my long black hair with the evening breeze. The flowers in the field next door had closed their petals for the night. I thought I caught a glimpse of red run in between the long stems, but as I blinked it was gone. My hands held the scissors I'd found in the kitchen and, as I walked towards the bathroom mirror, I prepared myself for the first cut. Each snip sent my raven locks to the floor, bit by bit my hair became shorter, finally resting on my shoulders. Change was no longer resigned to the inside of my body, my once long face took on a prettiness that had been hidden. Freckles now sat proudly across my nose and where pale cheeks once sunk into my skull, now sat two shiny red apples. I gathered up the hair from the floor and made my way back to my room and tucked the long black hair under the mattress. Mother's old teddy stared at me with one eye, he now had a part of me to keep him company once I was finally gone from here. The small key in my pocket fitted snugly into the wardrobe door, with a creak and groan it opened. A moth flew out, fluttered around the room for a few seconds then made its way to the light shade. It flapped furiously as the heat of the bulb singed its wings, and finally it settled on a piece of unravelled brocade that was once stitched to the shade. At the bottom of the wardrobe was a large book, the red binding cracked and split as I picked it up. As soon as I saw the date embossed on the front, I realised it could have belonged to my Mother. Dated 1985, she would have been fourteen and still living here in this old house. Inside were the handwritten words, *"This diary belongs to Meredith Jones, if anyone reads this apart from me then you are a snoop.*"

My index finger traced over the words. I yearned for her to be standing in front of me speaking them out loud. If the police had traced the call then soon this would be possible. If she'd run away into the arms of a lover, then I would forgive her, as long as she was safe. Many of the pages were blank with just the odd scribble "*homework*", "*dentist*" or "*school holiday*", it was only when I got to December's pages that more details had been filled in. One page dated Friday 6th, December, read:

The snow is so deep today, Mom and Dad said I could have the day off school. Her anger is getting worse, but we knew it would happen. At least Winter gives her a rest from the horrid birds and Dad is more able to calm her down. I miss my friends in the Winter, the food I leave out gets eaten, but I haven't seen Dusk for weeks. I hope he's ok, snuggled warm somewhere underground, maybe I'll see his cubs in the Spring.

The next day's entry:

I told Mom about the boy that had been following me. She screamed, furious that I hadn't told her before. Dad said he would call the police if it happened again, but I won't know until school on Monday, that's if the snow clears. I'm sure I saw him up on the cliff's edge in the Summer, every day he would be there looking out to sea. Perhaps I'm going crazy like Mom, I must get out of here as soon as I can; however I shall miss the meadow.

There were no other entries until Tuesday 24th of December:

Spent the day with Sara, we went to the old boathouse and exchanged presents. One day I will earn enough money and buy it. I will turn it back to how it should be and sail a boat across the estuary. When we walked back along the path towards the castle I saw that boy again. He walked past us and smiled. Sara said she fancied him, but I said he wasn't my type. He looked more like a girl with his bright red curls and a lot older than us. Sara thought he looked about 18, but I'm useless with ages. I didn't tell Mom and Dad, he'd not followed me since early December, she would have gone into a rage again and Christmas would be spoilt. I hate it here in the Winter, there's nothing to do and it's too cold to paint outside. I shall be glad when the guests return, Mother's always more pleasant to be around. The lilac tree never flowers and I worry that in the Spring it will die away. I shall wear its colour forever in memory of the first sighting of my friends. I would go mad without Sara. I tell her everything, even about Mom. She calms me down and always tells me it's not my Mother's fault. I'm so glad my Choosing was of land and not air.

This was the last entry. I held the diary close to my breast, these few precious words had taken me into my Mother's mind. This was when the first real tear fell; a slow trickle ran down my rosy cheeks and the taste of salt finally entered my mouth. I savoured every droplet. Spinning around the room, I held the diary high up in the air, my dancing partner made of the rarest paper. Sara must hold answers to many questions, my Mother trusting her with her innermost secrets, and perhaps she knew where or what had happened to her.

The diary was now mine and, after carefully placing it inside the lining of my suitcase, I made my way downstairs. The whole house was still, my Grandmother no doubt in a deep sleep helped by the medication she desperately needed. The small notebook I had brought with me had all the contacts in case of an emergency. Sara's number was at the back of the book, it had never entered my mind she could be a key player in the unravelling puzzle before me.

At first I thought she wouldn't answer, but eventually I heard a voice. "Sara Keys, how can I help you?" Her Welsh accent was strong.

"Sara, it's Martha."

"Oh, Matty, I was hoping you'd give me a call."

"What do you know about foxes?" I asked.

There was a long pause, at first I thought she had hung up on me, but finally she whispered, "I think you'd best come and see me, don't you?"

Her answer was not of a vet whose knowledge of all creatures could help any nature lover, it was one of 'I think I know what you're asking'.

"Can I come over tomorrow, that's if Grandma's well enough?"

"Of course you can, you can't miss my house. It's painted bright pink, 13 Castle Road."

"Thank you, I'll see you sometime in the morning." Placing the receiver back, I quickly jotted down her address in my notebook. Tiredness had crept up on me and my Mother's bed was calling. I returned to my bedroom, the welcoming fresh air from the open window soon lulled me into a deep sleep. No longer scared of noises from non-existent demons, the night passed with a peaceful silence.

CHAPTER 17

Each grey strand had been carefully tied with velvet, the lipstick applied with precision. She had laid the breakfast table with a crisp white cloth, neatly placed cutlery had been arranged for my appearance. The smell of filter coffee brought back memories of home. Her misery had gone and I was adapting to her mood changes.

"Oh I like your hair, it suits you," she said, smiling, as she passed me an assortment of jams. Bacon and eggs were sizzling and spitting in a pan, reminding the old house of the once hungry guests awaiting their first meal of the day.

"I thought it was about time I had a change," I said, tucking into my first slice of toast.

Her wrists were covered with a long-sleeved pink T-shirt that was neatly tucked into her black trousers. The haggardness gone, softness had returned as she gracefully moved around the kitchen, her swan neck held high.

"How are you feeling today, Grandma?"

"I'm much better today, Martha, forget all about yesterday. Are you ready for some breakfast?"

She walked towards the cooker, humming the same familiar tune she had done on my arrival.

"How are your bruises?"

"Silly me, I forgot to tell you what happened. I stupidly left my pills here when I went out yesterday. They stop me feeling giddy and I was out much longer than expected. I lost my footing and tripped over some uneven paving stones, I went down with such a thud." She raised her eyes towards the ceiling, avoiding my gaze.

"Anyway, enough chat about me, what are you going to do today?"

"And the crows, why were you so scared of them?"

"What crows?"

I wanted to weep for her.

"It doesn't matter, Grandma, as long as you're feeling ok. I was thinking of cycling into Laugharne this morning, as long as that's alright with you?"

I would get answers from Sara.

"I must be a mind reader, I've put the bike out front ready for you. It's going to be a lovely day so you make the most of it. I will give Peter a call and ask him if he will come over and help weed the drive."

"But it's Sunday, Grandma."

"That won't make a difference to him, he's always keen to earn some extra money." She sniggered, passing me a plate of bacon and eggs. I still knew very little about him and wondered if he had any social life at all.

"How long have you known him?" I asked.

"Your breakfast's going cold," she replied.

Frustration began to rear up once more, her pleasant mood didn't stop her being irritating and avoiding my questions. I quickly ate in silence then returned back upstairs to get my rucksack and sketchbook. I called out goodbye before closing the front door behind me, but she didn't reply. There was one crow on the roof; like a black sentinel it gazed down towards me, no doubt awaiting for its comrades to join him. My Grandmother seemed a magnet to all winged creatures, perhaps attracted to her unstable mind. No doubt when I returned her mood would have changed again, disturbed by the presence of their black feathers. I hesitated before grabbing the handlebars. Looking up at the roof, I wondered if I should go back inside to check if she was ok.

It was just one silly crow, hardly an army of terror.

My feet slowly turned the pedals, sending gravel scattering into the conifers either side, leaving a ridge in the driveway behind me. On the horizon, the sun was low, so low I wanted to reach out and bring it down towards me. I began to pick up speed down the hill towards Pendine. Exhilaration flooded through my body, the early morning breeze blew gently through my hair, I felt glad to be alive, even the urge to sing passed through my lips. The mesmerising orange glow drawing my eyes away from the road.

SCCCRREEECCH…….

The smell of burning rubber against the tarmac rose like a dirty perfume, bringing my eyes back to the car heading towards me. Breaking hard, my back wheel wobbled as I struggled to hold on. I watched in slow motion as the car swerved to avoid me, coming to a halt just inches from my front wheel.

"Don't you know there's a speed limit around here you stupid idiot?"

The window of the car slowly wound down. I didn't recognise him at first. In exchange for the ageing uniform I'd seen yesterday was a dark blue denim shirt and baseball cap, he looked nowhere near retirement.

"You and that bike are not meant to be, Miss James." It was PC Matthews.

"And you should know better than to speed along a country lane officer," I retorted.

"Well, as you no doubt can tell, I was on my way to see you." He passed a large brown envelope through the car window.

"Here's your phone, sadly we couldn't find any message from your Mother or any incoming call from that number. I managed to charge it though." He smiled, bringing more youth to his face.

I snatched the envelope ripping it open with a frenzy, my faithful time keeper had been charged and it had a signal. Not believing his words, I pressed through the menu, frantically searching the history. Lizzie's text was there, but my Mother's call had gone.

"That's impossible! It was there."

"I'm sorry, Martha, I was hoping this would be a major lead. It would have been great to wrap up my last week and help solve such a case."

He must have deleted the call log, opting for a few easy days where he could laze about the station drinking coffee, while lying to the others about how much he would miss the job.

I felt sick, all proof she was alive had been taken away from me. Leaning forward across my handlebars I spilled out my venom.

"Listen here you lazy son of a bitch, from now on I will not tell the police anything." My neck was purple with rage.

"Miss James, I understand it's been a traumatic year for you, but…." He spoke softly, his cap resting on the steering wheel.

"Get out of my way," I interrupted.

"I see the Welsh sun is suiting you, Miss James."

"Did you not hear what I said?" I pushed my front wheel against his car door, I was prepared to ram it.

He sighed.

"Just move over to the side slightly and I'll drive up to the house then turn round, listen out for me on the way back though. We don't want you having any more accidents, do we?"

Climbing off my bike I steered it towards the hedge. The risk of him calling in on my Grandmother and telling lies about me was too great. I decided to wait until I could hear his car come back down and pass me. If he didn't appear within a few minutes then I would cycle back up. A minute or so passed before I heard the car engine behind me. Pressing my body close into the thicket, I watched as he slowly descended down the hill. It was then I noticed a small wooden gate on the opposite side of the road; overgrown with privet and brambles, its broken frame was being supported by the hedges either side.

Placing my phone in my jeans pocket and the brown envelope in the basket, I slowly pushed the bike towards the gate, still listening out in case he decided to change his mind and come back. As I approached, I could see a blaze of colour above the wooden frame, it was the entrance to the meadow of flowers I had seen from my bedroom window. If this was a way in, then later I would return and investigate. The word '*Chosen*' flooded back.

Soon I was back pedalling down towards the main road, knowing that the sea was nearby as the sound of gulls had returned. Pendine was still as busy, the air was deafening with children squabbling over who could run to the beach first. Gathering speed, the caravan park soon passed me in a green metallic blur. I turned right on to the cycle path, my wheels gave an occasional jolt as they dipped into tiny worn out potholes. The Welsh rain had hammered down and broken up the concrete making my body judder. I passed through a small village, its lazy houses oblivious to the holiday invasion two miles up the road. The scorching sun beat down upon my head as I picked up momentum. I rarely used my bike at home, even though my Mother said '*I was a natural*'. When I returned home, I vowed to myself I would drag it from the garage and challenge her to a race.

Eventually the cycle path came to an end; ahead of me stood the wire fence to the Ministry of Defence. I was forced back onto the road. I passed the last village before I came to the bend towards the hill going down into Laugharne. Taking my feet off the pedals, I freewheeled down the hill, my wheels spinning faster and faster with the estuary breeze drawing me closer to its heart. As I turned the corner into the town, I noticed how all the houses were different colours. From pastel pink to baby blue they nestled close to each other, almost blending into one rainbow of stone. Sweat ran into my eyes, my hands were too firmly fixed to the handlebars to wipe them. I touched the brakes as I neared the bottom of the hill, slowing me down in time to see the estuary on my right. The tide was turning, the small car park and pathway to the estuary were covered in rippling water that moved to and fro as the sun pulled it back to its source. Birds flew in the sky in anticipation of what would be left for them once the sandbanks were exposed; soon they would feast on mussels and crabs. The road narrowed before me. I climbed off my bike and pushed it along the path next to the castle. An elderly man sat on a bench, housed in the old bus shelter that stood in front of the castle walls. He looked up at me as I pushed my bike past him.

"Morning," he said, as he tipped his trilby away from his head.

I acknowledged his greeting with a nod and said "Can you tell me the way to Castle Road please?" I attempted a smile, but my novice lips struggled to move.

"If you follow the path round and up the hill, it's the first road on the left." He pointed his old wrinkled finger towards the end of the castle wall and smiled. His toothless mouth opened wide, letting out a chuckle, "I wish I was young enough to get on a bike again, much cheaper than buses."

Thanking him, I continued past the old wall and turned up the steep hill. I pushed my bike onto the cobbled pavement, past a babbling brook that ran behind the base of the castle. On the opposite side was the sign for Castle Road, the old iron sign embedded into the wall of a small cafe on the corner. People were sat outside on tables and chairs, drinking coffee and taking photos of the brook below them. Cameras filled me with dread, over the past year so many of them had tried to capture a tear. I counted the numbers on the doors; eventually I came to 13. The small cottage stood detached.

I took a sharp intake of breath.

It was all lilac, every inch of stone had been freshly painted with my Mother's colour and I felt a sense of betrayal that Sara had stolen it. A hound's head made of brass hung from the front door, its ears drooped down to form a handle and it clattered under my hands as I banged furiously to let her know I was here. Immediately the sound of barking and snarling came from behind the door, dogs could be heard running up and down the hallway, her voice trying to calm them down.

"Be quiet!" she commanded.

Slowly, the front door opened, sending a bloodhound careering towards me, nearly knocking me backwards into the road.

"Back here now!" she screamed as the dog sniffed around my feet, its tail not wagging, but lowered between its back legs. Eventually, he turned and ran back into the house, followed by a smaller dog who bounded after him.

"I'm sorry about that, Martha, come on in. I'll lock them away so they don't bother you. We don't want you having an attack."

In my keenness to get out this morning, I'd completely forgotten to pack my antihistamines or my inhaler.

*What was happening to this girl who lived her life through routine,
I was now living dangerously and I was loving every minute.*

I stood in the hallway, the odour of wet dog filled the air.

"You said it was pink."

Sara looked bemused "What's pink?"

"The house."

"Oh stupid me, I'm so used to the old colour I forgot it's been
newly painted." She paused, "I thought you would like it."

I did not reply.

"Leave your bike outside, no-one will touch it, you can trust
people with your life around here." She smiled as she ushered the
dogs into a room leading off the hallway. Much to their disgust, the
dogs were now locked away; they let out a few whimpers before
becoming silent.

"They won't bother you now, come on through to the kitchen."
She turned and led me down the hallway. The low ceiling brushed
against her hair as she ducked under a large oak beam that framed
the entrance to her kitchen. Chaos was everywhere, paperwork was
strewn across a long scrubbed pine table, an ashtray overflowed
with cigarette butts. On one wall a Welsh dresser displayed a variety
of blue and white plates, thick with dust.

"Excuse the mess, housework's not my priority." She stepped
towards me, her arms outstretched, dog biscuits crunched beneath
her feet.

"Give me a hug, eh?"

I hesitantly moved towards her, being in the arms of a woman I
barely knew made me feel slightly uncomfortable. As I got closer,
the familiarity of her perfume disorientated me, taking me back to
my Mother's arms.

Her hands gently brushed back my hair and she said softly "It
suits you."

"You're wearing the same perfume as my Mother." I backed away.

"Oh no, your Mother wore the same perfume as me, come sit
down, we have much to talk about." She threw her head back and
laughed.

Turning to one of the pine benches, she sat down; her fingers tapped against the wood of the only space on the table, calling me to join her. Her face appeared neither female or male, but rather neutral androgynous features resembling sculptured marble. I imagined her in a museum, a statue of white, standing on a stone plinth, tall and godlike, but without sexuality.

As I sat down opposite her, I glanced up, a large oil painting hung on the wall opposite. The scene depicted men on horseback, their red jackets flowing behind them. A pack of hounds ran at the hooves of these large brown beasts, their snarling lips pulled back exposing razor sharp teeth. She was studying me.

"It's a cruel sport."

"What is?" I asked.

"Fox hunting, thankfully it doesn't happen as much around here as it used to."

"Why would they hunt a fox?" I scoured the painting searching for a figure that resembled the beautiful creature I had encountered the day before, "What do they do with it when they catch it?"

Sara held out her hand to grasp mine. "You want answers to many things don't you? Your life has been thrown into turmoil since Meredith went missing and she has left a great hole in all our hearts, I would like to help answer what I can."

"Let's start with foxes; you're a vet so tell me everything you know." I took my hand away, she had not gained my full trust yet and she would never fill my Mother's shoes.

"I take it you've had an encounter with this creature?"

I nodded.

She rose from the bench and walked towards the Welsh dresser; opening up one of the cupboards she produced a large leather-bound book. At first I thought it was an old family bible, similar to one I had seen at home, but as Sara brought it closer to me, I realised this was far different. The heaviness of its large silver clasps made a thump as she placed it on the table in front on me. There were no letters indicating what was to be inside, only three large silver rings intertwined, deeply embossed into the dark brown leather cover.

"Open it," she said, "this is yours now."

I flicked open the two hinges that held the old velum paper, pulling back the cover.

I gasped.

Written in gold were the words *'Trinity of the Chosen'*.

CHAPTER 18

"Hear the cries of Black Winged skies
Or taste the salt of waters deep
Pray your words remain on earth
For creatures thoughts bring deadly sleep"

I nervously turned the first page, an engraved etching showed a young girl standing high upon a cliff edge, her arms raised upwards, the sky full of gulls swooping down towards her. Her face was pale and ghostly, a lost soul waiting to plunge into the deep water beneath her. Yellow hair had been overlaid with gilt making her stand out from the page, a 3D image that you could touch and hold. At the bottom of the picture, in gold script, was the word '*Air*'. The next page showed an elderly woman walking through a wood, the lush green leaves of the trees had fallen around her and many had placed themselves across her body forming a woodland gown that was at one with nature. On her shoulder sat a blackbird, his yellow beak open as if calling for her. Again the word '*Air*' was inscribed at the bottom of the page. The next few pictures were all of similar scenarios, women of different ages surrounded by a variety of different birds.

Then the pictures began to change, one was of a woman swimming deep within blue water, a shoal of silver fish danced around her small frame, her long black hair floated above the water. Other pictures showed girls submerged in water, surrounded by creatures of the deep. Under each engraving was the word '*Water*'.

The last few pages of the book were of animals, one showed a female child lying in a field of lambs, her eyes closed, tears running down her cheeks. The next was a girl riding bareback on a chestnut horse, her arms draped around his neck and she was whispering into his ear. I stared at the last picture in disbelief. A large lilac tree sprawled across the page and underneath the branches sat a red haired child. She was smiling and in her arms was a young fox. Underneath was written '*Earth*'. I caressed the surface of the paper, my fingers outlining her red ringlets, this was the most beautiful picture of all.

"Isn't it magical?" I heard her say. I had been so entranced I had completely forgotten her presence.

"Where did you get it from?" I asked.

"It arrived here the day after your Mother went missing, with it was a letter which I will read to you."

"What? You have had a letter all this time and you never told me." I slammed down the cover of the book, the fury in my eyes bore deep into her.

"Give it to me now. I want to read it."

Sara's hands trembled as she passed me an envelope. I tore it open wondering if this would finally give me the answers to where my Mother was.

Dearest Sara,

I am coming back to Pendine, Father made such a mess of his estate and Mother has become so ill she cannot cope any longer. Her insanity fills me with fear, not only for her safety, but mine. Word was sent from Midnight, through others of his kind, from field to field, over many miles, a message had been relayed. Finally, late one night I was paid a visit. My heart burst when I saw the creature. I very rarely see them where we live and sadly the ones I do see have suffered the fate of busy roads. He spoke to me through my mind, warning me that if I returned I may be in danger. I questioned why, but he didn't know. However, my dear Sara, I have got some really exciting news; the old boathouse where we had so much fun is now up for sale. I was contacted by a man who said he was the owner and he was happy to sell it to me for a fair price. I shall be meeting him when I return back to see my Mother. Just think, Sara, finally I can restore this old building back to its former glory. I've already been working on sketches and plans. Stuart and Martha don't know yet, I want it to be a surprise and our holiday home, eventually I may be able to persuade Stuart to give up his job and move to Laugharne. I miss you so much, my dear friend, soon I'm hoping we can spend more time together. I have sent this book, you know how much it means to me, will you keep it safe as the words of Midnight's messenger have been eating away at me. If anything should happen, please give it to Martha if at any point she comes to Wales. You will know the time when things must be explained.

Love you with all my heart and look forward to seeing you soon.

Your loving friend,

Meredith

My mouth gaped open at the words in front of me '*If anything should happen*'. I looked up towards Sara, tears were welling in her eyes.

"The police never mentioned this, I hope to God you told them." My voice screamed at her, ringing down the hallway, alarming the dogs with my anger at their owner. They barked back in unison, warning me they were there to guard her.

She lowered her head.

"I couldn't, Martha, do you really think they would have believed me if I had told them the truth? I have spent months trying to find out who owns the old boathouse and no-one can give me answers. I would give anything to have her back, I loved her Matty, as much as you."

"What truth? You are just like my Grandmother always talking in riddles." I stood clutching the letter tightly, I needed to leave and call Charlie.

"Wait, let me explain, you are special like your Mother, you are one of the 'Chosen'."

"If I hear that bloody word CHOSEN one more time, I swear to God, I will make someone suffer."

"Please Martha, come and sit back down and things will become clearer."

"No more riddles though?"

She nodded.

"I swear that if you have prevented the police from doing their job, I will make sure you get locked up."

She clasped her hands together, "I beg you, what I am about to tell you may not seem rational, but it is the truth."

I waited.

"The land around Pendine and Laugharne is special, some families are selected to bear a gift. All females that are born within these families eventually become *Chosen*. When the child is born, it can neither laugh nor cry or show any emotion, just like you Martha, and your Mother," she paused, "yes even your Grandmother."

I shook my head.

"That's impossible."

"The three elements air, water and earth contain creatures who have the power to communicate with a *Chosen* one. They each select who will be a portal to their minds, this frees the girl or woman and, eventually, with their help she changes, finally removing the shackles of misery. Your Grandmother was chosen by '*Air*', but sadly the ability to laugh didn't last long. The birds of the sky helped love and cherish everything around her, but this comes with a price, for every thought that a bird has can be heard by the mind of a *Chosen* one. Can you imagine, Martha hearing the thoughts of a flock of birds, in shock at the treachery that man does to man across the world. They see war zones, famine and horrors that we cannot imagine. Your Grandmother suffered the worst fate by being chosen by air, eventually this gift to communicate drove her to insanity. Imagine your mind so full of voices, all you wish for is a sky of silence."

"And what about water, how is that possible?"

"Very few are chosen by water, usually the daughters of fisherman who sail out with their fathers to catch food for the table. It is only when a girl touches the water or swims deep within the sea that she can be *Chosen*. Many innocent girls have drowned on a summer's swim, not knowing that a million voices would enter their head. Panic can strike, so most mothers keep their daughters away from the water's edge.

"So, you are saying my Mother was chosen by creatures of the earth?"

"Yes, but the fox selected your Mother first and I have a feeling it has selected you too, as you mentioned you had an encounter with them earlier." She tilted her head to one side, "Has it?"

I was not willing to offer any information, she had withheld such a precious letter that could have helped find my Mother months ago. If this was true and I was to be *Chosen,* then it was my secret alone and I would be the one to find out why.

I looked blank.

"No, I stumbled across an injured one yesterday and wondered if there was anything that could be done to help it."

Her eyes narrowed. "Are you sure you have had no communication, it is important Matty?"

"I am sure and to be honest, I don't believe in this nonsense, it is a book of fairy tales and a myth that has grown from people who have nothing better to do with their lives."

The sound of barking dogs was making it difficult to continue our conversation.

"I need some fresh air, I'm going for a walk."

"Let me come with you, I can bring the dogs, we could walk down to the estuary and maybe talk some more."

"May I use your phone?" I asked, "I just need to check my Grandmother is ok."

"Of course you can, feel free, it's on the wall in the kitchen. I will go and get the dogs and see you outside."

I waited until she disappeared then picked up the phone; dialling my Grandmother I waited.

"Hi, it's Martha, I am just checking how you are and did Peter come?"

"I am fine," she said. Her voice sounded childlike, "he is such a lovely boy and has worked so hard this morning. Will you be back for supper?"

"I'm not sure what time I'll be back, but make sure Peter stays with you."

She put the receiver down before I had chance to say goodbye. Sara appeared, her two dogs stood either side, muzzled and pulling on their leads.

"Pull the door behind you," she said, striding down the hallway.

When we arrived at the car park, the estuary was a blaze of feathers, the tide had gone out leaving them a feast. She led me over a small bridge along a path beside the castle. We paused briefly as a jackdaw landed in front of us. I wondered what stories he could tell.

We continued along a paved path; in the distance I could see a house, it appeared to be jutting out of the cliffside as if floating in the air.

"If we walk further down there's a bench where we can sit and the dogs can have a run around."

I grabbed her arm turning her towards me.

"That house up there, is that the boathouse Mother mentioned?"

"No, that's Dylan's, the other is much further down the estuary."

Disappointed I muttered "oh."

Eventually we came to a bench, its legs sodden by the tide, Dylan's house was looming nearer. Steep stone steps ran up towards the suspended house.

"It's worth a visit," she said as she sat down and unleashed the dogs. I prayed they would not come sniffing round my feet, thankfully the excitement of being free sent them darting towards the water's edge.

"I've heard Dylan mentioned before, tell me more about him."

"All you need to know is he was a drunkard Welsh poet that made the boathouse his home for many years. The town is proud of the beauty around it, but many come here to visit purely on account of Dylan's history. It's only when they see the view they realise this soil and water has more to offer than a few lines in a poem."

I made a mental note and promised myself that when I returned home I would research the works of this man, but today was not the day for a history lesson.

"Your Grandmother was born around here, did you know that?" Sara said.

"No, I thought she was born in Tenby?"

"Meredith told me your Grandmother moved to Tenby as a teenager, she never knew why, but that's how she met your Grandfather. Perhaps she thought she could escape the voices of birds, sadly there is no escape and Tenby is alive with them."

"If this nonsense is true, why didn't my Mother tell me?"

Sara paused for a while. "If you are *Chosen,* it is forbidden to discuss this gift until your child is *Chosen* herself."

"And you? Are you *Chosen?*"

"How I wish I had been. The reason I became a vet was in the hope that one day an animal brought before me would read my thoughts and answer. I've also known from the time I was born that I could laugh; therefore, I do not have the '*gift*'. It can take many years to find out who you will be chosen by. There are tales of women who have been visited on their deathbeds; maybe by a mouse that enters their bedroom and the first smile they take shows on their face before their last breath leaves them."

I sensed a deep sadness in her voice.

"Are you sure you don't feel different since you have been here and you have not been visited?"

"I am sure." I looked at her directly, there was no way I would tell her the truth. "I want to go to the old boathouse, how do I get there?"

"As I said, it's much further down Martha, and the paths are overgrown, the only remnants of its original standing are a few terracotta tiles and broken wood."

"If someone offered to sell it to my Mother then surely the police could find out."

"I have tried and failed and your Mother also tried over the years as she wanted to make it her home, but time passed and she became busy with her job; eventually she gave up. All she was able to find out was the firm of solicitors it was registered under; however they could not reveal the name of their client."

She has obviously made more effort than I thought, perhaps I could trust her.

"If anyone can find out, it would be my Father." I grabbed Sara's hand and squeezed it tightly.

I was sure once he knew Mother had arranged to meet the owner he would scour every land registration until he found the truth.

"Let's hope he can, Matty." She squeezed my hand back in return.

"I just need a few minutes on my own Sara, I won't be a minute."

Getting up from the bench, I walked a few more yards towards the boathouse. The nearer I got the more imposing it became, its small windows and slated roof reminded me of a doll's house I once had. Playing childhood games never came easy to me, so it stayed in a corner of my bedroom collecting dust. Then one day it disappeared, I never missed it so I never asked where it went. The path had now come to an end, I could see the large rocks and stones that formed a climbing platform to the steps leading up to the boathouse. I fumbled in my pocket for my phone, to my relief it showed a signal, this beautiful remote place had given me a lifeline to my Father. I dialled his number, not giving a damn about the time zones, even if it robbed him of sleep. The familiar answer phone told me to leave a message.

"Call me tonight on the house phone, it's important."

"Is everything ok?" Sara called. I turned to see her now a few feet away, the dogs were back on the lead, tugging to go back to the water. The hound bared his teeth, snarling as I walked towards her.

"Stop it, I don't know what's got into you today." She yanked back the leads, they let out a whimper then lay flat on the ground, ignoring me as I approached.

"Yes, everything's fine, do you want to head back?"

"I think the heat's getting to the dogs so I'd best take them home. I could meet you at the bistro. I'm not sure about you, but I'm starving." She smiled, her tall figure stood like a goddess framed by the scenery behind her.

"Mother loved you, didn't she?"

"Yes and I loved her, see you in about an hour?"

She walked away, taking giant steps back up the path towards the castle wall. The dogs by her side, wagging their tails furiously as they occasionally gazed up for approval. Soon she had disappeared from sight and I was alone, back on the bench gazing out towards the water. A small boat bobbed gently up and down in the distance, its white mast cast a long shadow across the rippling surface. A figure appeared at the helm, it was too far away to make out any features, but the frame looked like a man and he was waving. I looked around to see if anyone else was on the path, but there was only me. I raised my arms to wave back, but the figure disappeared, the distant hum of the engine started and slowly it glided through the water, passing the boathouse and out of view.

CHAPTER 19

I heard a bell chime twice, it reminded me that time was becoming less important, and the air around me was changing every fibre of my body. The bistro was bustling with visitors, one table outside was spare. I sat down waiting for Sara to return. Gwyneth came skipping through the open door, happiness radiated from her as she waltzed in and out of the tables taking orders. I was in no doubt, she must be *Chosen*. The owls inside the bistro were an indication that she had been dealt a short straw. Madness would eventually gnaw away at her spirit, turning her ashen, leaving her with no will to live. She stepped towards me, as if I was a long lost friend.

"Hi Martha, lovely to see you back again. Your hair is so pretty and you've caught the sun." She pointed towards my arms, which were now golden brown.

"I cut it myself, it's not the neatest of hairstyles, but it will do for now." My monotonous tone was leaving me, I almost sounded happy.

"Well, it looks lovely. What can I get you?"

"Just an orange juice please."

She left me to gaze at the comings and goings across the square, people keen to make their way to see Dylan's house; paying homage to his legacy. I could see Sara making her way towards me, she had changed from her casual shorts and blouse, into an ankle length white linen dress. She was that sculptured goddess I had conjured up, the museum begging to add her to their collection.

"Ah, there you are, sorry if I took a bit longer." She sat down, the sweet perfume had been reapplied.

"I've brought the truck down, your bike's in the back, so I can give you a lift when you're ready."

I was grateful to hear these words, I was not looking forward to riding back in the scorching heat.

"Thank you. What would you like to eat?" I asked.

"My treat, they do great toasted sandwiches here. I'll go inside and catch Gwyneth before she gets too busy; the sun sure brings out the visitors in Laugharne."

She left me briefly before returning with two glasses of wine.

"Thought you might like some vino." Her laugh was more infectious than Lizzie's, even on her best days.

"I'm not old enough to drink."

"Rubbish, you look much older than you are. However…" Her voice tapered away and I realised she was studying me.

I felt uncomfortable as I knew what was running through her head. I was physically changing, a light had been lit in my eyes, bringing me youth. She passed me the glass, as I took my first sip I anticipated an exotic combination of fruits to warm my mouth; all that entered was vinegar and remnants of old orchards.

She took a large gulp, smacking her lips she said, "It takes a while to get used to."

I placed my glass down on the table, deciding one bitter sip was enough for me.

"I couldn't help but notice the bump on your head."

"I fell off my bike."

"Matty, I want you to know you can always talk to me about anything, and I mean ANYTHING."

I wondered what she was alluding to.

"Matty, you can tell me if your Grandmother's becoming violent."

"She's not." I snapped.

Now her eyes were boring through mine, searching for the glimmer of a lie. A few uncomfortable minutes passed before she spoke again. She chatted about her job and the animals that came before her; sick and in need of human care. Her voice changed to sadness as she spoke about the ones that were beyond her help. These creatures, who whispered into the ears of their *Chosen,* would be destroyed with the aid of a needle. Their owners would be left to mourn and search for another of its kind. Gwyneth appeared and she fell silent. I asked Sara how she first met my Mother, presuming it would have been when they started school. I was taken aback when she informed me it was on the beach at Pendine.

"I remember it well, the small red haired child, who still hadn't learned to laugh. Your Grandparents had taken her down to the beach, and she had wandered off. I found her by the rocks, her pale face blank and lost, this was before she had been *Chosen*."

"Were you with your parents?" I asked.

"No, I am three years older than Meredith, and I knew the beach well. I took her small hand and led her back to her parents, never thinking we would become best of friends."

"I thought you were the same age, Mother never said."

"Age does not determine friendship, Matty. When she started school I continued to take care of her, until I knew she'd been picked. She changed like you will, our friendship became stronger each day; we were inseparable up until the time she left for University. I stayed in Wales to study, but your Mother needed to get away from the illness that was devouring your Grandmother." She turned her face towards the estuary, a single tear trickled down her white cheek; she brushed it away as quickly as it appeared.

We ate in silence, the heat of the sun now beating down on two women who shared a loss. Time had stood still for me, this small town held so much charm and I wondered why my Mother would want to leave. The so-called 'madness' was a small price to pay to be a part of such beauty.

"I best get you back, the book and letter are in the car, take care of them, Matty."

I wanted to stay here forever, sketching in my mind every fold and turn of the estuary, but I knew my Grandmother needed me.

"Can I come and see you again?" I asked.

"Anytime, let's go." Her smile returned.

We ambled back to the car park, her hand holding mine, as if I were that lost child on the beach. No more words were spoken on the journey back to Pendine, occasionally she patted my hand, a wave of affection came over me and I wanted to kiss her cheek. Eventually, we turned up the hill towards the house, passing the gate that I would visit when the sun went down.

"Did you get the food delivery I sent?" She said as we pulled up the driveway.

"Was that you?" I exclaimed. "Grandmother was convinced it was me."

She said nothing for a moment.

"We can't have you starving whilst you're here, she'd have you living off birdseed." She gave me her goddess like smile as the car came to a halt. "I see she's sprucing the place up a bit, with the help of Peter of course."

Peter's van was parked outside the front door, hanging baskets full of geraniums now hung either side of its wooden frame.

I sensed a hint of sarcasm in her voice, "Do you know him?"

"I know his Father, we were once engaged, but it wasn't meant to be." Her lost expression stopped me from asking more. Raising her hand I gently kissed it, her loneliness obvious and I promised to myself she would no longer feel solitude.

"You have me now."

She smiled and putting her arms around me, she whispered softly, "And you have me."

I waited as she took my bike out of the back of her truck, she handed me the book, saying the letter had been tucked inside. It wasn't until the sound of her engine became a distant hum that I stepped inside, I quickly made my way upstairs to my room. I placed the book on the dressing table. There seemed little point in hiding things anymore. Whatever was to be my future could not be changed. Out of the window I could see her, sat on a garden chair, her hands clasped tightly together as she stared down towards the lilac tree. Steel step ladders straddled the trunk as Peter's strong legs firmly balanced on the rungs. His torso was immersed amongst the branches, he was snipping away at the dead wood. The carefully shaped tree was now coming to life, sending out green shoots towards the sun. I made my way back downstairs; my heart began to quicken as I neared the back door. There was no doubting the fact he was handsome, his face still with a boyish charm, but the bone structure of a man.

She was humming, swaying backwards and forwards as the notes rose to a peak, oblivious to my presence.

"Are you ok, Grandma?"

She stared out vacantly, grey hair cascaded across her face like winter waves. Peter heard my words and swiftly descended the ladder, the familiarity of his smile gnawed away at my memory; I was sure we had met before, but this was impossible. My life had only ever consisted of Lizzie and my Parents, and of course, time, minutes and seconds, that once controlled all that I did.

He strode towards me, faded denim clothing a body, that somehow I yearned for.

"Hi Matty, you been to see Dylan's place then?"

"No, I went to visit a friend."

"She's no friend." She turned towards me, her mouth twisted into a snarl.

Peter mouthed, "Can I have a quiet word?"

As he came closer, the smell of soil and sweat merged together forming a toxic cologne, my cheeks reddened to scarlet.

He whispered in my ear, "She's been fine up until an hour ago, chatting away happily."

"What happened?"

"We were out here eating sandwiches when she started pointing up to the roof, screaming and pulling at her hair. I wondered what the hell was up there."

"And what was up there?"

"Nothing, I thought the house had caught fire or the roof had collapsed. There were just two old crows sat pecking at the tiles, she was going crazy."

I glanced up to check the roof, there was no sign of the crows.

"Did you want to get off, I can take care of her now?"

"Trying to get rid of me, eh?" His moss stained hands brushed a trickle of sweat that ran down his brow.

"Stay for a bit longer then, I'm just going for a shower." I turned away, not wanting him to see my longing. This was all too new for me to cope with, this place and the people who were reinventing Martha.

I made my way back to the house, desperate for cool water to run over my body. Whilst the shower ran, I rifled through my wardrobe, searching for something that would direct his eyes towards me. I cursed as my hands touched the plain T-shirts, then I suddenly remembered the silk blouse that Lizzie had smuggled in. It hung in the wardrobe, a gift from her in the hope I might wear it to impress a young Welsh man. How was I to tell her that her prayers had been answered? She would no doubt think I'd either taken to drink or suffered sunstroke. My hair was still wet, as I tucked the pale pink silk into a fresh pair of jeans. The freckles that were dotted across my nose had blended into one, forming a golden glow across my face. I would go barefoot back into the garden with my sketchbook, to capture the last of the afternoon rays. When I returned she was nowhere to be seen, Peter was tugging at decaying wood from the tree.

"Where's she gone?" I called.

"For a rest, said for you not to worry." His voice muffled between the growth of new leaves.

I sat down on the grass, my pencil brushed against the paper with ease, neither firm nor rigid, it flowed until the tree took form across the page. This was unlike any of my previous drawings, free of all discipline. My fingers trembled as I tried to steady the lead. My Mother was working through my hands, from smudges, to the shading of the bark, I was becoming an artist.

"Well, let's have a look then." He was back down the ladder, remnants of twigs had settled in his hair. I turned the book towards him, not afraid to show what I'd captured.

"That's beautiful, you're really talented!" He exclaimed.

There was still no smile, but pride burst from my heart. I was no longer a prisoner of art. He came and sat down beside me, his shoulders slightly pressing against my arms; my body now tingling.

"I need to ask a favour, Peter."

"Ah, so you do want me to take you to Dylan's house then?"

"I have to go somewhere at sunset, and I'm worried about leaving her alone."

"Where are you going? You shouldn't really be wandering off on your own in the evening."

"I can't say, but I will be safe, will you stay until I come back?"

"Let's strike a deal, I will stay if you let me take you down to the beach tonight. You will be able to see the beauty of the sands, without the distraction of deck chairs and screaming children. It is a scene that I am sure you would like to draw."

Nervously, I nodded, this was a fair bargain. However, being alone with a man I barely knew, filled me with slight apprehension. It was true, I was attracted to him, but it was still early days for me to share an emotion I had only just discovered. The air was becoming cooler, refreshing us both as we sat in silence. I still knew very little about him, he'd told me nothing about his personal life; perhaps he had a girlfriend or was married. I looked down at the third finger of his left hand. There was no ring.

An hour must have passed, Peter had gathered up his tools and I tried to call Lizzie from the phone in the hall. I desperately wanted to tell her about him and my Grandmother, and the beauty of Laugharne. After several attempts my heart sank, she was probably too busy with her spotty faced boyfriend. The door under the stairs to the cellar was open, I made my way down the steps to check on my Grandmother, she was lying on the bed awake, her eyes fixed to the ceiling, motionless, for one moment I thought she had died. I pressed my ear against her chest to check her breathing, it was slow, but consistent, she stretched out her hand holding mine, tracing the outline of my fingers with hers.

"I am going out for a bit Grandma, I won't be long. You will understand why I have to go."

She acknowledged my words with a single blink, then continued to gaze up at the cold damp ceiling. I kissed her forehead before returning back upstairs. Peter had settled himself down in the kitchen, he had made himself a cup of tea and was reading a book on the history of Welsh roses.

"I thought all roses were the same."

"Anything that comes from Wales is special and different." He winked at me, my cheeks began to flush once more.

Closing the front door behind me, I walked down the gravel drive. The sun had now changed from orange to red, the light casting a shadow before me as I walked. In the distance I heard a cry, no longer feeling scared or threatened, I quickened my pace down the hill. The old gate came in to view, overgrown and neglected it called for me to climb over. I hauled myself across and entered the field of flowers.

CHAPTER 20

Each flower bent away from me, as my footsteps took me forward; parting before me, as if they knew I was coming. The harshness of my jeans occasionally bruised a cornflower, I hoped I would be forgiven. The birds, who whispered words to my Grandmother, had unknowingly scattered a botanical ocean. Scarlet as a child's blood, poppies swayed towards each other, I made sure the soles of my trainers caused them no harm. I wanted Peter to be with me, holding my hand and breathing in their perfume, but he was back at the house, caring for a women he barely knew. It was selfish of me I know, but I needed to find out if the Trinity existed. I thought about his father and wondered if the flowers cowered in horror when he entered with his gun held under his arm, awaiting an innocent rabbit to be shredded with lead, then taken home for to be served on a blue and white plate.

As I walked further in, the ground became softer, flowers were now replaced with grass, the occasional clump intertwined with soft strands of fur from rabbits, who had hoped to see another day. Before me was a clearing of grass, completely circular, cut out with perfection. I wandered into the middle, the sun was now gone, and I was alone in silence. Then I heard the cry, shrieking and screaming towards me, getting louder and louder as the seconds passed. I wanted to run, but my legs became heavy, like a dream you can't awake from in the deepest sleep. Was this the sound of a creature that was so beautiful? Why had it been cursed with a noise that turned blood cold? A shiver ran down my spine. Then it stopped, silence returned once more. The wall of flowers gently moved and made way for him, he sprang forwards, running towards me, as if I was his Master. My chest tightened, I took a deep breath in, trying to remind myself that this animal hadn't harmed me before. But what if I'd been fooled? This animal was wild, not tame like a dog, who would wag its tail and lick my face.

What if my asthma returned? My chest would become so tight, all oxygen would leave my body, I would eventually drift into a state of unconsciousness, only to be found the next day, punctured with wounds from a hungry fox.

He stopped at the edge of the circle, his amber eyes fixed on my every movement. Dark brown ears tipped with wisps of black, twitched in anticipation of any threat.

"You have come."

The words boomed in my head, I placed my hands across my ears, fearing my ear drums would burst and send blood running through my fingers.

"STOP IT!" I screamed.

He sat there, his head tilted on one side inquisitively, not understanding.

"Do not use your mouth."

Again the noise screamed through my brain. I lay back on the grass, my hands pressed so deep in my skull, I feared I may crush it. I could feel him next to me, his warm fur brushing against my arm, he now lay by my side.

"Clear your mind of all thoughts." This time softer, more soothing. *"We have learned to help, we will not allow the mind sickness to control you, but you must listen to what I say."*

Slowly taking my hands away from my ears, I placed them on his soft coat, my fingers buried deep within the golden top layer. I tried to empty my mind of everything that had happened to me, forgetting even my Mother, I lay there awaiting his instructions.

"Others will soon come, you must concentrate only on words from one of our kind at a time, then speak through your mind, for we will not hear words from your lips."

His smell was pungent, old soil and corn had seeped through his coat, cold winter storms battered by rain were his cologne, but it didn't bother me. My own smell would be strange to him, skin washed by shower gels made of chemicals, sun-lotion smoothing my tanned skin. He might also smell sadness, alone and unhappy, the girl who never laughed.

"*I feel your loss.*"

Yes, he could read my mind, as I could his. His pain was far worse than mine, betrayal flowed from him. His family murdered by guns and hounds, chased over green land that should have been there to protect him. My fingers dug deeper into his coat, I knew soon my eyes would stream, my throat would tighten like a vice, but it would be a small price to pay. We connected as one, and I didn't want to let him go. My mind was so entangled with his I was unaware that we had been joined by others.

"*They are here, remember to only open your mind to one of our kind at a time.*"

Twenty or more foxes were stood around the circle, some young, their coats still dense with cub fur, their eyes bright and innocent. Others were aged, old wounds and scars mapped across their faces; their snouts grey and silver. A young fox walked towards me, in her mouth was a cub yet a few weeks old. He wriggled and yelped between her mouth, desperately waiting to be put down on the soft earth. She placed him at my feet, looking up at me for approval at what she had produced.

"*Save us.*" Her words were frail and tired.

An elderly fox limped towards me, his back leg dragging behind, probably broken many years ago and never healed.

"*You are your Mother's daughter, the one you call Meredith?*" This was a question, his voice was hesitant and unsure. His eyes nervously darted backwards and forwards across the meadow. I could feel the fear.

Concentrating hard, I focused on his weary eyes.

"Yes, I am Martha, daughter of Meredith."

The fox cub was now rolling at my feet, chewing and tugging at the laces on my trainers. I picked him up, holding him close against my chin, his small snout buried into my neck. I couldn't hear his thoughts, but I sensed his innocence. He wanted to play and run free through the flowers, unaware there could be dangers before him.

Midnight arose from my side, standing tall like a sentinel of all foxes.

"I am Midnight, my Father's Fathers and all generations before me knew your Mother."

The others bowed their heads in recognition, he was magnificent and they honoured him. My eyes remained clear, the swelling and itching I so dreaded did not come. My lungs sucked in the evening air, it was pure and free of allergies that a few minutes ago, I feared would kill me.

"How can I save you?" My thoughts directed towards all of them.

"Your Mother said there was a place, a safe haven for us to go and she would take us there. A place where men could not harm us."

Sadness filled every fibre in me, my Mother who loved me with such tenderness, had also shared her affection with these animals. It was them who had turned her into a woman who embraced life.

"Will you help me change?" I asked.

"You are already changing." This time, the words came from a fox I hadn't seen before. She gingerly stepped towards me, her sleek body finally rested next to Midnight.

He placed his nose against hers, embracing for a few seconds, the companion he hoped would bear him offspring. The love was overpowering, not like human; deeper, intense and cruel. I envied the connection between them.

"She's gone. I don't know where she is. I'm sorry, but I haven't a clue where this safe place is, unless…" I paused, thinking of my Mother desperately wanting to buy the old boathouse in Laugharne.

Midnight spoke again, *"The day your Mother's Father was put beneath the soil, she said she had news, she told us she would return and lead us there."*

"Tell her about the man." These words had a different tone, full of distress, coming from the vixen who had held the cub.

Midnight raised his head towards me. *"The man who shoots in this field was watching your Mother. One of our kind saw him at the gathering of those who buried your Grandfather. He spoke to her, but we know not what he said. He kills our kind, and we fear as your Mother hasn't returned, he may have harmed her. We sent warning through our brothers and sisters over many miles, but we do not know if she heard the message."*

I felt sick to the stomach, bile collected at the back of my throat. I spat it onto the ground with disgust.

"Yes, she had a visit. I've got a letter she wrote, telling me about the warning. She did return."

"This does not bode well." The young vixen moved closer towards me, her head lowered to the ground. *"You know the son of this man."*

My head began to spin, I was overcome with nausea at the thought Peter's Father had been stalking my Mother. Did he have an obsession with her?

"My Mother has contacted me. She is alive."

Midnight gently took the cub away from my arms and carried him back to his Mother. He turned towards me, *"That is not possible, she would have come to us. She is gone."*

"I'm telling you the truth."

Then all their voices came into my head, questions flooded in, some doubting and others accusing me of lying. I felt my knees buckle underneath me, my head exploding with sounds and screeches that would surely destroy me.

"STOP!" Midnight's shriek drowned out the others, one by one they became silent. *"If this is true, then why has she not visited us?"* He rested his paw against my arm.

"Why me?"

The tears flowed like never before, at last I was grieving for my loss. The empty hole in my life would never be filled. The call I'd had off her was gone. She would have contacted me by now. The realisation she could be dead was too much to cope with. One by one I felt them on me, licking my tears away with tongues as rough as sandpaper. Their warm fur blanketed me from the outside world,

I was wearing a coat of foxes, but one that was living. My hands stretched out to touch them, they embraced me in a golden haze amongst this field of flowers.

"I will find out more." I whispered in-between sobs.

Midnight's eyes darkened, his love entered through me like a river that had burst its banks, sweeping into every vein of my body. I lay there, letting them tell me stories of their lives, how my Mother would keep watch, stealing food from my Grandmother and running wild with them until the stars appeared. The young vixen told me how her future would be, giving birth to offspring that Midnight would hunt for. Her destiny was to be his mate, and each of her thoughts were full of hope.

They heard the sound of death before me, one single crack soaring across the field. The insects, that had bedded down for the night under the petals of poppies, rose in a cloud of wings. I lay there, my face flat on the ground, my heart pounded into the grass like a drum. I stretched my fingers out to feel the warmth of their fur, grasping out to hold them near me. Desperation hit, only the blades of grass touched my fingers. I moved my head slowly from side to side, searching the low ground for a sight of fur. This single crack was not from a shotgun, it was from a machine that propelled one deadly fire. Like a rifle on a shooting range, it had been directed at me. Still lying flat, I fumbled in my pocket for my phone, praying it would have a signal, so I could call for help. I dragged it towards my face, but there was nothing. The black screen only reflected the horror in my eyes. My breathing became faster, putting my hand across my mouth to stifle the noise, I lay there waiting for whatever fate was before me.

Minutes passed and I slowly pulled myself up to a crouching position. I gazed at the wall of flowers, crawling through them would be my only option. If I was to risk standing and making a run for it, the blackness of my hair would be a bullseye for the gun. My chin rested deep into my chest, it was then I saw the splatters. Scarlet droplets of fresh blood were scattered on my silk blouse, my chest anticipated the searing pain that no doubt would come from the wound underneath. There was nothing, no throbbing or burning, I waited for it to come. More time passed, my eyes stared down expecting to see more blood ooze into the silk. Clutching at clumps of grass, I turned myself round to face the other side of the circle. She was there, lying where my feet had been. The young vixen, who had lovingly nuzzled up to Midnight, was motionless. A single gunshot wound had pierced her chest; exact and aimed at her small beating heart. She was still warm, my hands reached out to move her closer to me. The last few seconds of her thoughts came rushing through me, I felt pain like no other, she knew that she was slipping away. By the time I crawled next to her, she had gone. Her mind was blank, no more dreaming of time with Midnight and the offspring they would produce. Tears of rage fell from me, they dripped onto her snowy breast, paling the liquid that seeped from it. No longer caring if I was heard, my screams raged across the meadow, cursing all around me. Pounding the air with my fist, I cried out over and over again.

"You bastard! Come and get me!"

My endless screams echoed through the petals, I felt the flowers recoil in fear. Now I understood hatred, the urge to kill with revenge was overwhelming, another emotion I'd never experienced, and one that I would thrive on, until I choked the last breath from the perpetrator of her death. In the distance I heard the low rumble of an engine, perhaps it was the killer driving away, but it sounded as if it was getting nearer. Eventually the roar of diesel came to a halt near to the edge of the field.

Peter's voice was calling me, but I couldn't leave her, his desperate shouts becoming louder. Eventually, I could see him running towards me.

"Help me!" I cried out.

His strides trampled down everything in his path, but I was beyond caring.

"Oh my God, Martha!" His wide eyes scanned every inch of my body, looking at the blood splatters on my clothes. My arms began to shake with the weight of the body, I was sure that I would drop her at any moment. The shock of what had just happened spilled out from me in a jumble of nonsense.

"She's… She's… Your father… He's… He's killed…"

Peter raced forward and before I could say anymore, he took her from my arms.

"Matty, I need to know, are you hurt?"

Yes I was hurt, not from a gunshot, but from the knife that had cut out my heart.

"He's killed her." I spat the words out at him, contempt in every syllable.

"Who has?"

"Don't tell me you don't know. I was beginning to trust you!"

"You think my Father's done this, don't you? Look at the wound, Matty. It's from a rifle, not a shotgun. Dad hasn't got a rifle, plus he's away in London."

I didn't trust anyone anymore, his Father could have a stockpile of guns for all I knew.

I called out in the hope they would hear me. "I will take you to the safe place. Revenge will be sweet."

"Who are you talking to?"

Stone-faced I turned back towards him, I could see even with his strength, he was finding it difficult to hold her.

"Take me back. She needs to be buried."

CHAPTER 21

When we returned she was awake, humming to herself in the kitchen; the smell of freshly baked cakes could not overpower the stench of blood on my clothes. As soon as she looked at me, she understood my pain and held me close. Her cheek squeezed against mine, the face powder no longer disgusted me as it clung to my skin.

"I'm so sorry, Matty. You know where to bury her." She whispered into my ear.

Under the lilac tree was the only place she should go. Darkness made it difficult for Peter to see as his spade dug deep into the grass. Grandmother was stood in the kitchen doorway, she watched as we lowered her down into the ground.

When I asked if Father had called, she just shook her head. He wasn't interested in me, or what was going on in Wales, his career was far more important; I began to hate him as much as Peter's Father.

Even when the first cut was made in the grass, she never objected, she just stood watching us bury an animal that her daughter had loved. Peter kept silent. His futile attempts on the way back from the field, trying to convince me of his Father's innocence, had fallen on deaf ears.

When the last piece of turf was finally trodden down on the makeshift grave, he lay the spade against the trunk, and stared up towards the stars. Swollen buds had begun to form from the new shoots, the tree was coming back to life, yet casting a shadow of death at the base of its trunk. I caressed the bark hoping it would hear my thoughts. Peter threw his head back towards the night's sky.

"It's a beautiful night." His eyes focused on the largest star right above our heads, the one my Mother had often pointed out to me, saying Venus was the Goddess of Love.

"Not for some, Peter."

"Dad will be back tomorrow, speak to him, Matty. I promise you, he never did this."

"Is it too late to go to Pendine?" I wanted to get away from this burial site; my heart too broken to stay around.

"I'll take you, go and get a jumper though, it's getting cold." The blood splatters had now dried a dark brown, giving me a chill that was far greater than the air around me.

I quickly returned wrapped in a warm red sweater. Peter was sat in the van waiting for me, he smelled of freshly dug soil and death. My body ached with tiredness, but I knew if I went to sleep I would be haunted by nightmares. As he drove down the hill, I looked out towards the old gate, wondering if Midnight had returned looking for her. I hoped he would forgive me for taking her away.

As we arrived into Pendine, Peter took a right-hand turn away from the seafront. A small narrow dust track led up towards the cliff way. The van's wheels bumped against the uneven surface of this makeshift road. When we reached the top, he turned into a small car park that stood overlooking the cliff.

He got out and walked to the edge, looking back waiting for me to join him. Total blackness was around us, I could barely make out his outline against the night sky. Slowly, I made my way forward, tripping on a large stone that had crumbled from the cliff edge. I stood beside him and stared out towards the sea. The darkness of the sky and water merged into one.

"I love it up here, I can think straight when things are going badly."

I felt his arm brush against mine, the warmth of his body getting closer.

"Tell me about your family."

He took a deep breath in and paused a while before answering.

"You're not the only one to have lost someone, Martha. My Mom died when I was three. Dad had met her in London, not long after he'd moved from Wales."

My eyes had become accustomed to the dark. I caught a glimpse of a tear.

"We stayed in London for a couple of years after she'd died, but Dad missed the countryside. The city wasn't really for him and he'd made a truck load of money from buying up houses and renovating them."

"Did you know your Dad was engaged to my Mom's friend, Sara?"

He spun around, we were so close to the edge I feared he would topple over, I grabbed his jacket and pulled him back.

"You seem to know more about him than I do!"

"That's all I know, apart from the fact that he likes to kill things." I barked.

"You've got him all wrong, he's a kind man who wouldn't harm anything. Shooting rabbits is a way of life round here. It's not as if he does it for fun. They eat crops that people need to live on."

"And foxes?"

"Why would he kill them? They keep the rabbit population down stupid." He turned to face me, I could feel his breath on my lips.

"And my Mother, how well did he know her?"

He drew back.

"He knows your Grandmother well, he helped out many times when your Grandfather became sick. Mainly in the house, as your Gran had lost interest in the garden. As for knowing your Mother, I don't know, but I don't like what you're getting at."

He knew I was thinking his Father may have killed my Mother, I was more or less calling him a murderer.

"I don't know anything about you, apart from your name."

"What do you want to know? I'm eighteen and live just outside Laugharne. I split up with my girlfriend three months ago and now I am stuck babysitting a strange girl who asks too many questions."

So he was with me out of pity, childminding a girl whom he found obnoxious. I raised my hand to slap him hard across his face, but he grabbed my wrist before I had the chance.

"Stop this, Martha. I know you've got good reason to be hurt and hate the world, but we're not all evil. Have you ever thought your Mother may have just gone off somewhere, fed up with her life back home and met someone else? Perhaps she wanted a new life of her own." He let go of my wrist, stepping away from the cliff, leaving me dumbstruck.

Could she have done this? Was she so unhappy with my Father and I? I was hardly the perfect daughter.

Remembering the argument she'd had with my Father the night before she left, I realised this was a possibility. Tears welled up in my eyes, I bit my lip hard to get them to stop.

"Why did you split with your girlfriend?"

"All she seemed bothered about were birds, reading about them and talking about how fascinating they were. Apart from her job in the bistro in Laugharne, she wasn't interested in anything else, apart from things with feathers." He was now smiling, flapping his arms and strutting around the car park like a cockerel. This bizarre sight almost made the corners of my mouth turn upwards.

"I've met Gwyneth, she seems nice."

"Yeah, she is, if you make squawking sounds... squawk... SQUAWK!"

I looked back out to the sea and listened to the gentle waves slap against the rocks below. He came up behind me, his hands gently resting on my shoulders.

"Can't we be friends, Matty?" Pushing his hands down, he turned me around to face him, wide pale blue eyes stared hard into mine, waiting for me to answer. The overpowering feeling to kiss him rushed through me and my lips touched his before he had chance to blink. I'd read about love, gushing fountains of emotions making your head spin and your stomach knot. This kiss felt wrong in so many ways, his lips were cold and unresponsive. I quickly stepped away from him, confused as to why it felt so unnatural. He wiped his lips with the back of his hand, I could see he felt the same way. There were no fireworks or sparks flying around us, we were two strangers thrown together out of circumstance.

"I err… I'm… err… so…" My words trailed off into a whisper, the night around me hid the burning on my cheeks.

"No need to say sorry, I'm quite flattered."

He placed his arms around me, no longer sending excitement, it gave me a feeling of friendship and protection.

"Come on, let's get you home. Hope you don't mind me saying, but you could do with a shower." His words were meant to tease, but they were true. My time with them had covered my skin with an earthy odour, the smell of death seeping through every pore.

He guided me back across the car park, my eyes swollen from endless tears over the last few hours and sleep was calling me.

As he drove back down towards the seafront he asked, "Why were you in the meadow?"

It was pointless telling him the truth and I still wasn't sure if he would go running back to tell his Father.

"I wanted to see the flowers and maybe paint them before I go back home."

He turned to face me, his eyes narrowed in disbelief. "You could have gone anytime to do that."

Silence was my only answer and thankfully he asked no more questions. The house was in darkness when we arrived, apart from the dim lamp in the hallway, it looked in mourning.

Putting the key in the front door I turned towards him.

"Will you be back tomorrow?"

He stretched his hand out and brushed my cheek. "Yes, but I have to pick Dad up from Tenby station first thing. Your Grandmother's asked me to whitewash the walls of the house and he's offered to help. She seems keen to clean the place up. It must be your influence on her, Matty." His grin had returned, wide and welcoming.

"See you tomorrow then."

I didn't look back, my legs were weary as I climbed the stairs. Each step weighing me down. I clung onto the banister, heaving myself up to the final one before the landing. A cold chill had entered my room and, with ease, I closed the window shut. As I took one final look down the garden, I saw a small shape against the tree. I could see his silhouette, it was Midnight laying over the newly dug grave. Placing my hands against the cold glass, I prayed he could see me, but he never looked up. The lump in my throat choked my sobs as I slumped on the bed, my head buried in the old feather pillow. I thought back to the time when I couldn't cry and longed to be that same girl again, emotionless and cold, but at least my heart never broke.

Sleep came quickly and so did the dreams. I was running through the meadow, my heart frantically pounding to get away from a man. He was tall like Peter, his coal-black eyes boring into the back of my head as he got closer. The smell of his breath was on my neck, stale and rank from rotting animals, he placed his mouth down on the flesh of my shoulder. The sudden sound of gunshot sent me spiralling down to the ground. I awoke with a jolt, my arms flailing out as I was falling. I felt her body next to me, my arm banged against her face making her wince with pain.

"It's just a dream, Martha. Go back to sleep."

Grandmother's frail body pressed closer to mine, she was now my guardian for the next few hours, as sleep returned without nightmares.

CHAPTER 22

I must have been about seven the last time I'd slept past midday on a Monday. Chickenpox had splattered my pale skin, the frustration of not being allowed to get up and see if they were dotted in order came flooding back.

"Martha, you need to stay in bed, you're not well." My Mother's Welsh lilt somehow had a medicinal quality that immediately made you feel better.

"But what if they are uneven, I need to count them!"

She was used to these outbursts, never flinching or showing frustration with what must have been a difficult child to deal with. My phone told me the time was 12:32. Grandmother was no longer beside me, but the indentation in the mattress showed she had been there. My eyes felt gritty and sore, this new emotion of grief had taken its toll on them; my unwashed skin filled the bedroom with the odour of foxes. Slowly I dragged my body out of bed and made my way to the bathroom. The cracked mirror reflected the redness in my eyes, multiplying them by ten, as I moved around the room. My face had changed forever, physical signs of suntanned skin blending with sorrow had metamorphosed me into a woman. The cool shower water washed away remnants of the day before, fox hairs swirled around, finally resting in the plug hole beneath my feet. The air was humid and oppressive, even after I had dressed and put a clean T-shirt and jeans on, I felt the sweat gathering at the nape of my neck.

I could hear a voice from downstairs, loud and booming it made its way up the three flights of stairs to my room. At first I thought it was Peter talking in the hallway, but this voice was deeper and more mature. I wasn't in the mood for meeting new people. I wondered if it would be possible to climb out of my bedroom window and somehow hang on to the old ivy that crept all over the back of the house. I could use it as a rope, then lower myself to the ground and sneak out through the back gate. The steel ladder that Peter had brought to scale the back of the house lay flat on the lawn, out of reach for any escape that would save me. This ridiculous notion soon went, I saw the drop I would have to make, so with much reticence I made my way downstairs. The voice was coming from the back room, she was nervously laughing in between the deep bellows of her companion. Despite my efforts to tread each step down without making a sound, the old staircase gave me away.

"Martha, you're up, come on through." I stood in the hallway, cursing her under my breath and the locked front door ahead of me. "MARTHA!" she was irritated by my dawdling and I could tell the madness in her was back.

The temperature drop hit me immediately as I took my first step in, musty velvet curtains still shut out all light and sound, protecting her from the birds who whispered words. Standing beside her was a man, he was not much taller than her, his hair a mop of red curls peppered with silver. This booming voice I'd heard from upstairs now seemed farcical, coming from such a small frame. He looked in his late forties or early fifties, but guessing ages was somewhat of a low priority in my life. Back home I paid no attention to faces, apart from those of my Mother and Father. He was staring at me, his mouth wide in a familiar grin that showed the same teeth as his son.

"I am Michael, pleased to meet you at last. Peter's told me all about you." His stretched out hand opened to shake mine, but I recoiled back into the doorway.

Anger boiled in my stomach, spilling up into my throat sending out words of venom. "I know who you are, you evil son of a bitch. You get a kick out of killing innocent creatures."

The smile soon disappeared, his eyes widened with disbelief at my outburst. The petite frame of my Grandmother grew in the dim lit room as she launched towards me, her eyes flashed with anger, gripping my arm she pulled me back into the cold air.

"You apologise at once, do you hear me?" She screamed.

Grabbing her bony fingers with my other hand, I squeezed tight until she let out a cry. I felt her manicured nails recoil from my skin as she let out another gasp of pain. I felt no remorse, only power, as she stumbled back into her chair. The expression of shock on his face filled me with satisfaction.

"What the hell?" he said. I thought the purple veins that had appeared on his forehead would now burst, but I wasn't afraid.

"Hell is where you're going, for what you've done."

Peter's voice came echoing behind me, "Jesus, Matty. What's going on?"

I turned towards him, now there was no mistake that the man with my Grandmother was Peter's Father. They shared the same canvas of genetics, but Peter had been more carefully painted.

"Dad, will you tell her that you were in London yesterday, she's convinced you shot a fox in the meadow."

He nodded and slowly stepped towards me, the smell of expensive aftershave masking the musty smell from the room.

"Peter's already told me what happened and I'm truly sorry, but I wasn't the one who shot the fox. I think you owe your Grandmother an apology."

It was then I noticed his emerald green eyes, they looked far to old for his face, as they glared at me to believe him.

Pushing my way past Peter I shouted out, "I owe her nothing."

"Matty, we need to talk, now is not the time, but I promise we will later," she begged.

Fumbling in my pocket for the front door key, I made my escape quickly onto the drive. My bike was still against the conifers, the coldness of the handlebars numbing my hands as I made my way down the hill. The air was damp with forthcoming rain. I couldn't risk returning for my jacket, my rage would cause destruction. The wood creaked underneath me as I climbed over into the meadow, I made my way back to the circle. Flowers crushed beneath my feet, I hadn't time to worry about them, I needed to save Midnight and all of his kind. I called out for him, waiting under dark clouds that now gathered above my head. I should have realised he wouldn't come, why should he? I'd betrayed him like all others of my kind that walked on two legs. Filled with despair and fighting more tears, I returned to my bike. The seat was wet from the large droplets that were falling. I made my way hastily down towards Pendine, my feet pounded on the pedals, I needed to be as far away from the house as possible. Silhouetted against a large grey cloud was a crow, it swooped down towards me then flew up towards the hill.

By the time I reached the main road of Pendine, I was soaked through, my hands struggled to wipe away the rain from my eyes. It was impossible to see what was in front of me. A car honked its horn as my wheels wobbled towards it, I quickly turned onto the pavement before it had chance to clip the back of my bike. All the tourists had gone, they must have known the weather was changing, deciding to stay dry in their caravans or guest houses. Parents would offer colouring books and board games to their crying offspring, in the hope they would silence them.

The cafe would give me chance to dry off, by the time I'd had a hot chocolate and eaten a bacon sandwich the rain may have eased and I could think about where I should go next. Steamy windows made it impossible to see inside, rain cascaded down the poster of my missing Mother, her face looked ghostly as she peered through glass. I leant my bike against the window and walked in, the bell above the door jangled as I slammed it behind me. All the visitors of Pendine appeared to be sheltering here, their chattering drowned out by the hissing of the expresso machine behind the counter. The elderly woman in charge of the coffee machine looked flustered, "I won't be a minute."

"Just bring her order over, I'll settle the bill." A voice shouted from behind me, it was PC Matthews who looked delighted to see my bedraggled face.

Is there no escape from anyone, especially those I distrust?

"Tell her what you want, then come and join us, we're over there." He pointed his finger to a table tucked away in the corner.

Gwyneth was sat on a chair, staring into space, her chin resting in one hand and the other holding a milkshake. I looked around, desperate for someone to get up from another table, leaving me to dry off in solitude. I waited a while, a crack of thunder confirmed I had no other choice than to sit with her. I ordered a sandwich and hot chocolate, then reluctantly followed Matthews over to the table. My feet squelched against the lino floor, leaving muddy tread marks from my trainers, my jeans sodden with rain.

"I'll pay for my own," I said stonily.

"Nonsense, give me chance to spend the first of my pension."

"I gather you've met my grandfather before."

Gwyneth laughed softly.

"Is everyone related to each other round here?" I retorted.

"I keep her out of trouble," Matthews chimed in.

"Gramps looks after everyone." She looked at him fondly.

The waitress slammed down my bacon sandwich, grunting under her breath that my hot chocolate would soon be over.

Matthews expression changed and his brow furrowed. "So, Martha, have you had anymore phone calls?"

I shook my head, even if I had I wasn't going to tell him.

"We're all so sorry about your Mom, I hope you hear some good news soon." Gwyneth stretched out her hand across the table to touch mine. I quickly retracted it, tucking it under the table. Her cheeks flushed with embarrassment, as she sucked on the straw from her milkshake.

I ate in silence.

Minutes dragged as Matthews and Gwyneth chatted happily to each other. When the last mouthful slid down my throat, he rose from the table.

"Right, I'll go and pay then. Best get off, and don't forget to let me know if you hear anything else."

He walked towards the counter, slamming a handful of coins down before leaving. I hoped she would follow. Her brown eyes were only on me, the inquisitive expression on her face told me she wasn't going anywhere.

"I get the feeling you don't trust him, he's a good man and would help if he could."

"I don't need any help."

"I know you've been *Chosen*. I can see how much you've changed."

I glanced around to see if anyone had heard her. On the opposite corner an elderly lady smiled, then resumed stroking her terrier that sat patiently on her lap.

"And you?" I whispered.

She gave a nod before sucking up the remaining milk in her glass.

"You're allowed to talk about it once you're selected."

"So the birds have *Chosen* you?"

She didn't answer for a moment, her dark eyes stared around then finally met mine.

"We have no choice, but to accept our destiny."

There was no doubt she was beautiful, just like the birds who told of their adventures, her free spirit shone above her empty glass.

"Peter told me you were seeing each other."

"For a time, but it's difficult for another person to understand the life we have to lead. He's a good man and deserves to meet someone less complicated."

"What about his Father? Is he a good man?"

She shrugged her shoulders, "I don't know him well, but he seems ok, why?"

"No reason."

"So when do you go back home?"

"Soon. My Father will be back in the next few days to collect me." I knew this may not be true, his lack of contact could mean he was avoiding telling me he was staying on longer, but I tried to sound convincing.

I somehow got the feeling she knew I was lying, the clue lay in her sceptical smile. I asked her polite questions about her job in Laugharne, hoping that she would soon get bored of the chit chat and leave me alone. She delighted in telling me gossip about the woman who worked at the bistro, who had a sordid affair with a local shopkeeper, and that she may eventually run off with him. The vibration of my phone, thankfully, interrupted the continuing saga.

I slipped my hands into my jeans pocket, placing it on my lap out of her view.

This did not stop her trying, craning her neck as far as it would go, she tittered, "Boyfriend?"

"No, my Father."

This satisfied her curiosity, she continued on with her hypothesis that the woman would no doubt have another affair and leave the poor shopkeeper heartbroken. My eyes glanced down to the screen, it wasn't my Father. My hands trembled as I read the text.

Martha, it's Mom, have you got this?

Looking up at Gwyneth, I nodded in acknowledgement of her story. My hands under the table blindly typed, *Yes.*

"Where's the toilet, Gwyn?"

She pointed to a door to the right of the counter, watching me as I hurried towards it, my phone back in my pocket. I slammed the door, bolting it before I looked at the screen.

Matty, you must do as I say. Promise me you won't tell anyone you've heard off me.

My fingers sped across the screen.

I promise. Please Mom, tell me where you are?

I heard the door handle of the toilet door turn.

"I won't be a minute," I called out.

A disgruntled mother's voice could be heard, asking her child to hold on a bit longer and cursing the fact there was only one toilet.

Meet me at the old boathouse tomorrow at eight o'clock, don't tell anyone.

It was too late, the child was now crying and saying how sorry she was for the accident and could she go home. Flushing the toilet and opening the door my eyes avoided the glare of her mother, as I quickly brushed past them. I made my way back to Gwyneth, my phone securely in my pocket.

"I don't think she's very happy with you." She smiled.

"It's raining outside, no-one will notice the child's got wet pants." Her cheeks flushed with amusement, not realising I was being deadly serious.

"Have you ever been to the old boathouse?" I asked.

A police siren could be heard coming along the road outside the cafe, Gwyneth stopped to listen before she answered.

"You mean the old ferry house? Yes, a few times. Why?"

"Just wondered."

"It's hard to get to, most of the pathways are gone now." She leant over and touched my arm, "You sure you're ok? You've gone really pale." Before I had chance to give my excuse that I was tired, my phone vibrated again, this time ringing and not the 'bleep bleep' of a text. It was persistent, stopping occasionally then starting up again.

"You'd best answer that."

"I'll call them back."

It was no use, the noise had alerted people in the cafe to stop their chattering and stare at me until I answered. "Hello, who is it?"

"Christ Martha! Where the hell are you? You need to come back now!" Peter's voice sounded desperate, in the distance I could hear faint screams.

"The police are here, you must come back." The line clicked and the phone went dead, leaving me panic stricken with the realisation something was horribly wrong. I left Gwyneth open mouthed, she had no doubt heard his voice, but there was no time to say goodbye.

CHAPTER 23

The rain was now easing, but more charcoal clouds billowed above me as I approached the house. Replacing the noise of the pounding rain was a sound more terrifying than the cry of a fox. A thousand or more crows were calling together. No space could be seen between them, wing to wing they covered the roof in a blanket of crows. Two empty police cars sat parked on the drive, above them blue lights flashed. I ran through the open back gate, trying to catch my breath from the bike ride up the hill. Peter and his Father, along with four officers, were staring up towards the roof. My Grandmother was nowhere to be seen. I tried to call out to them, screaming for them to tell me where she was, but the noise drowned out my attempts to be heard. Peter's ladder leant against the wall, each rung contained carrion, intent on letting no-one step upwards. My eyes followed the ladders upwards, past where my bedroom window was and above. The rusty guttering swayed with the weight of the birds feet, as they bumped and nudged each other for space. It was then I saw her, long grey tendrils of hair flowing high in the air, both arms outstretched to the sky. Dressed all in black, she was their queen, commanding them to her. Bare feet straddled each side of the apex, her body leaning against the crumbling chimney breast. We watched as her mouth moved simultaneously with their cries, they were as one.

I raced over to the ladder, my fists flaying at the birds to get away; in a frenzy they pecked at my skin. Blood seeped across my knuckles, which only made them thirsty for more.

Peter cupped his hand over his mouth and shouted in my ear. "It's no use, Matty, we've tried. They won't let us near her."

I screamed towards the police, "HELP HER!"

Both officers were calling for assistance on their radios, their attempts futile above the noise. I drew back from the ladder, raising my leg as high as I could, I kicked against it. It swayed slowly, sending a few birds scattering, only to return with more savagery.

Michael looked ashen, his knees buckled underneath him as he fell to the ground, his face buried deep in his hands.

I violently tugged at his jacket sleeve. "The gun, get it."

His red curls shook from side to side, "I haven't got it with me."

Words of loathing spewed out towards him, this man I hated for killing creatures, knelt before me like a pathetic child. For once in his life the control over a trigger could do some good, but he'd left the killing machine behind. The deafening sound rose to an unbearable pitch, all of us clutching at our ears to protect what sanity we had left.

Then silence fell, sucking in all the air in one breath. She turned towards us, carried by their wings she hovered, her arms lowered by her side.

"Now it's time for me to fly!" she cried out.

It only took a few seconds before the sickening thud reached us. Her body lay at Michael's feet, broken and twisted, her lipstick smudged with a trickle of blood from the corner of her mouth. When my Mother had gone missing, I tried to imagine what death looked like. There were no broken bones or blood, only serenity and peace. A small river ran towards my trainers from her skull, I stepped back from the horror that was in front of me.

Now the police had silence. After checking her pulse there was no need to call for assistance, only for a doctor to pronounce her dead.

CHAPTER 24

"Martha... MARTHA... are you ok?"

I didn't answer, I was too busy trying to listen to the conversations coming from outside the back door.

"Please answer me, Martha. Can I get you a drink?" The quiver in his voice sounded desperate, and it was only irritation that made me answer.

"I don't want a bloody drink! You look as if you need one more than me, there is some whisky in the front room. Perhaps that will calm you down."

I was grateful that Peter left me alone for a minute, while he went in search of the liquid that might stop him trembling. I had been instructed to come back in the house while the ambulance took her away. He returned with a tumbler full of scotch.

"The crows... you saw them?"

He paused before taking a large gulp, "I can't explain what I saw, none of us can."

"Where's your Dad? And how come he was sobbing, he hardly knew her!"

"How can you be so cold? We have all just seen something horrific, but you seemed to be more affected by the death of that stupid fox." His glass was now empty and his hands shook violently. He turned his head towards the kitchen doorway, Michael was stood there ashen, his eyes now matching the redness of his hair.

"GET OUT!" I screamed.

"You can't stay here, Martha. Peter and I think it is best if you come back with us."

"I'm not going anywhere and definitely not with a murderous bastard like YOU!"

His voice became tentative, almost apologetic, "I'm just trying to help."

Before I had chance to hurl my chair at him, two police officers appeared behind him.

"Miss James, I gather you've been staying with your Grandmother for a few days." The younger of the two sat down at the kitchen table opposite me. I nodded anticipating his next question.

"Is there anyone you would like us to call?"

"You can try and get hold of my Father for me."

Peter piped up, "I can do that for you, Matty."

I spun my head towards him, my anger obvious to everyone in the room.

"We will try for you, Miss James, if you can give us his contact details."

"Has she gone now?" My quivering hands pushed my phone across the table showing my Father's mobile number.

"Yes," the other officer spoke up, his voice gruff and with little compassion. He slouched in the doorway and directed his uniformly sharp eyes towards me. "We found this outside, Miss James."

In his hand was a black phone charger, in a frenzy I raced towards him, my hands snatched the charger from his grasp. "That's mine. Where did you find it?"

"We found it under her body."

Revulsion took hold, it slipped through my fingers and clattered to the floor.

"I'll clean it for you, Matty." Peter picked it up and placed it on the kitchen worktop.

"What happens next?" I asked the younger officer.

"Let's wait until we've spoken to your Father, he can arrange to pick up the death certificate and sort out funeral arrangements."

"He's in Australia and not due back yet."

"I'm sure under the circumstances he'll come home, Martha. In the meantime, Peter and I can help." Michael was obviously not going to give up with his offers of support, no matter what looks of hatred I directed his way.

"The crows killed her." My frantic words did not appear to phase the officer opposite me, for one second I thought I detected the hint of a smile.

"The weather does strange things around here, Miss James. We gather the flock of birds that had settled on the roof were, no doubt, trying to shelter and regroup before taking flight again. I think it's purely coincidental that they were there when your Grandmother decided to take her own life."

"We all saw it, tell him Peter."

Peter walked over to me, his hand gently rested on my shoulder. "Matty, your Grandmother wasn't well, you know that. I think the officer's right and the crows just happened to be there."

I stared down at my knuckles, patches of dried blood told me his words were not true, I was surrounded by lies. Her madness was, no doubt, well known in the area. The loss of her husband and daughter tipping her over the edge, until finally she could take no more. This explanation seemed feasible and convincing, no doubt to the police, making it easy for them to fill in paperwork and leave without further investigation.

"I'll let you know as soon as we've got hold of your Father. Is there anyone you can stop with until he returns?"

I gave no chance for Michael to chime in. "Yes, my Mother's friend. I'll ring her." I wouldn't of course, but it seemed to satisfy him enough to get up and leave along with the other officer.

My eyes focused only on Peter, "You can both go now, I'll call you if I need to."

They glanced at each other, unsure of what to do next.

"GO!" I realised my scream may cause the officers to return, so added softly, "Please."

Finally, I was left alone to cry. I'd held back bitter tears for what seemed a lifetime. My head sank down onto the table, exhausted with pain and grief, my sobs became uncontrollable. I'd gone beyond caring who heard, I kicked out at the chair opposite me, and sent it flying across the floor. The glass that Peter had drunk from made a satisfying smash against the kitchen cupboard, sending shards across the worktop. Clearing up the destruction would give me something to do later, after all, I could do exactly what I wanted now, she was gone forever.

I never heard the cars leave, or Peter's van drive away. After what seemed like an hour, I decided to venture back out into the garden. There was no evidence of a death, no blood splatters or feathers; only the odd cigarette butt that Michael had discarded. Taking a deep breath in, I walked down towards the tree, the grass underneath it still felt uneven and disturbed from Peter's digging. The fragrance hit me immediately, light and sweet coming from above. Lilac flowers sprang from each branch in a glory of pastel mauve. This old dying tree had come to life in a matter of days, and was now paying homage to the creature that was buried beneath it. I lay back against the trunk, breathing in its life and perfume. Midnight soon came, I felt his presence well before I opened my eyes. His head stretched across my lap like a loyal dog wanting to be petted. My fingers sank deep into his fur, soothing away all pain that was within me. His thoughts no longer full of his loss, but for mine, wanting to comfort me in my time of need.

"*I shall find your safe haven.*" My mind said the words.

He answered me by burying his snout further into my lap, his odour and the flowers above made me heady, an intoxicating combination. He briefly left me, disappearing through the undergrowth of the hedge, only to return with a rabbit. It hung loosely from his mouth, no doubt a kill from earlier to feed himself for the day. He lowered it down to my feet, in an offering of sustenance that may cure my sadness. I almost smiled, this act of kindness touching my very soul. Unlike before, his head was empty of words, telepathy had been put aside. Now the sun was poking through the fading grey clouds, fighting for space to brighten up the day.

He followed me back inside, walking close beside me and pausing when I did to gaze back at the lilac tree. It seemed immense and dominated the garden, watching over everything that set foot on the soil around it. Midnight lay on the cold kitchen floor, studying me intensely as I cleared up each fragment of glass. After all remnants of my anger had been removed, I searched in every cupboard. Finally my hands rested on a tin of corned beef, I placed it on a plate and offered it to him. He devoured it within seconds then licked his lips in anticipation for more. He cocked his head to one side to see what my next movement would be. I gestured for him to follow me into the back room. The heavy curtains pulled back with ease, letting in a stream of light across the dingy walls. The chair, that only a few hours earlier supported my Grandmother, now stood empty. I sat down, tapping my lap, beckoning Midnight to sit by me. His eyes narrowed as he scanned the room, taking in the smells of human decay, his nose twitched from side to side. My eyes fell on the old writing desk, still strewn with papers and letters. They seemed aged and unopened, begging to be read by someone. I strolled across to look, while Midnight kept guard.

The paper knife that lay next to the first letter slid neatly across the top of the envelope.

Dearest Mother,

Why will you not reply to any of my letters? I need to understand, surely it's time the past is put behind us. I beg of you Mother, let us all be united before time takes you away.

Your loving M.

I studied the handwriting, perfectly neat using ink with precision, it flowed across the paper beautifully. My Mother was always proud of her writing, saying that computers robbed people of creativity. She obviously had no other option than to write, as technology was not allowed in this house. I opened another, again a similar demand that she respond to her letters. This one seemed more frantically written, the ink pressed hard into the paper with determination. It looked more masculine, but the swirls tagged onto the letter 's' were, no doubt, my Mother's.

None of this made any sense, who was she asking to meet? Surely if she hadn't replied my Mother would have called her? Perhaps they'd been written when she was at university. It was obvious by the age of the paper they were written some years ago. Holding the envelope up with my hand, I turned towards Midnight.

"My Mother is alive. I'm seeing her tomorrow."

He looked blankly at me, no recognition of my spoken words. I stepped towards him, my hand resting on his head.

"*She's not dead.*" This time I spoke with thoughts. I felt him flinch and take a step backwards, he let out a whimper before returning next to me.

"*How can this be?*"

"*Tomorrow is the day when I find out the truth. The safe haven will soon be yours for you and all your kind.*"

"*I must go with you.*"

"*No, I promised her I'd go alone.*" I could feel his hurt return. "*Soon Midnight, soon you will be safe and shall see her again.*"

"*Then I shall stay until you go.*"

He lay back on the floor and licked the last crumbs of corned beef from his paws. A few weeks ago I would have been gasping for breath, clutching for my inhaler to open my lungs, but now the air felt strangely clean. Calling Sara was next on my list, I wanted to speak with her first, before Michael spread the news. I owed her this, her kindness and love for my Mother had been my salvation. She took a while to answer, sounding out of breath from, no doubt, walking the dogs.

"Sara, it's Martha."

"Oh, hi Matty. How's things?"

"I've got some sad news." Without interruption, she let me recount every detail of my Grandmother's death. When I finally finished she whispered, "We knew it was only a matter of time before they came for her." Finally I had someone to talk to and believe me; not once did she question.

"Can I come over? I'm happy to stay."

"I'm fine, but thank you. I'm not alone." My eyes fell down towards Midnight who now was stood next to me.

"Who's with you?" I sensed that if I didn't reply quickly she would be over like a shot.

"Peter's staying."

"Oh, ok. Are you sure?"

"Honestly, and the police are contacting my Father. They may have more luck than me."

There was a pause, "I know your Gran never liked me and she was a difficult woman, but I wouldn't have wished this upon her."

"She was going to tell me something, but…" My words trailed off, realising that I would never speak to her again.

"The crows, they came to murder, Matty. She must have betrayed someone deeply for this to happen."

"What do you mean?"

"Being *Chosen* by air will always bring madness, that can't be stopped. Eventually death comes from natural causes, lack of sleep and a crazed mind reap through the body, until they draw their final breath. It is only then they find peace. A murder of crows only comes to those who betray."

"Betrayal seems everyone's middle name round here."

Before she had chance to answer, I made my excuses.

"Someone's at the door. I'll call you tomorrow."

A tinge of guilt hit, lying was becoming natural, spilling with ease off my tongue. I put the receiver down. The house was full of silence, apart from the patter of Midnight along the hallway. The sound of his steps, as he sniffed around the house, took away all loneliness. Gingerly, he ascended the stairs, stopping occasionally to take in the scent of those who may have used them. This old bleak house was bursting with hidden secrets, but like an overflowing dam, I felt it would soon break. I watched as his red tail disappeared out of sight, he seemed on a mission to uncover one of these secrets. Leaving him to investigate, I returned to the back room; the light now shone on all the surfaces. My finger dragged across the mantelpiece leaving a line of exposed oak, that had been hidden by dust. A prickling sensation ran across my shoulders, I felt someone was watching me. My eyes gazed up towards the mirror, the heavily carved birds looked poised to take flight from the frame. I darted back to the kitchen grabbing the table cloth. When I returned, I noticed a crack had appeared in one corner of the mirror. My hands carefully draped the cloth over it, covering up my reflection, along with what seemed like wings from nightmares. Before I returned home I would ask Peter to burn it, along with the examples of taxidermy in each bedroom above. Midnight soon returned, he nudged the back of my leg with his head.

"There is much unhappiness here, you must leave."

Kneeling down towards him, my hands stroked either side of his face *"Soon,"* I whispered.

Our mental conversation came to an abrupt end with the sound of banging on the front door. My heart sank, Sara no doubt felt that she should supervise me until Father's return. I opened it slightly, my excuse spilled out before I had chance to see who was standing there.

"Peter's just popped out."

"Funny that, I must have a double." In his hands he carried what seemed to be a box full of takeaway food.

"Thought you may need something to eat, I've been all the way to St Clears to get this."

He stepped closer, the smell from the box becoming stronger. His smile was beautiful, full of fun and immensely kind. The longing to put my arms around him returned. Oblivious that Midnight may be behind me, I opened the door wide. I glanced over his shoulder for his Father's shadow, then took a sigh of relief, he was on his own. Midnight had gone, fleeing out the backdoor, which from now on, would always be left open for him.

We hardly spoke as we sat eating. The fraught day had been brought back to normality with the simplicity of food, and silence. Peter cleared away, occasionally glancing over his shoulder to look at me.

"Did today really happen?" I finally spoke.

"Yes, and it was no-one's fault."

"Where's your Father gone?"

"He's taken the boat out onto the estuary, he said he needed to think."

"In Laugharne?"

"Yes."

"Will you take me there tomorrow evening?"

He folded his arms and leant back on the kitchen work surface, looking clumsy and awkward.

"On one condition, you let me stay here for the night."

"Ok, you can have any of the guest rooms and I only need dropping off."

His cheeks flushed, "I wasn't expecting to share a room with you."

Gazing down at the floor, I hoped the scorching in my cheeks was not mirroring his.

"Hope you don't mind me saying, Matty, but it sure smells of fox in this house."

My smile came naturally, like a mother giving birth to her first child. "Yes it does and I like it."

CHAPTER 25

I was running out of clean clothes, tomorrow was the day I would be reunited with my Mother and I wanted to look my best. While Peter returned home to get his overnight bag, I placed my silk blouse in the washing machine. After my futile attempts of hand-washing out the fox's blood stains, I succumbed to the power of the machine. Watching it spin in frothy soapsuds Mother's words came flooding back *"natural fabric should always be treated with respect"*. I hoped she would forgive me if it had faded or shrunk slightly, but blood was a powerful liquid to eliminate. I hung it on the line, the evening breeze sent it high in the air, a silk balloon desperate to fly high, but held down by wooden pegs.

By the time Peter had returned I'd washed and dried most of my remaining clothes, all hanging neatly in order ready to be packed away for my return home. She would come back with me, even the lover she may have met could perhaps be persuaded to return with her. After all, I was her only daughter and if he loved her then he could learn to love me. My Father would soon get over it, taking comfort in the fact that she was alive and no-one would ever point a finger at him again.

I stepped out into the garden, calling out for Midnight. The rabbit had now vanished from the base of the tree, he was probably in the meadow sharing each mouthful with the youngest of his group.

The evening was drawing in, all grey had lifted exposing a sky of deep azure blue. Soon the stars would look down on Wales, I mentally pictured them shining down on my Mother. The cold reality of my Grandmother lying on a morgue slab broke the image. I shuddered, her broken body and twisted neck was a sight that could never be erased, like the bullet hole in the fox. Death seemed to surround me, no matter what beautiful visions I tried to conjure up.

I returned to the house and picked up the keys from the back room to unlock a door on the first floor. I chose the room with the owl, the connection with Gwyneth may make him sleep easier. Its face seemed less menacing than the others, like a character from a children's book, this wise old bird was supervising and in charge of anyone who entered. I stroked his creamy soft feathers thinking he had only uttered words of wisdom into a *Chosen's* ears.

The roar of Peter's van could be heard coming up the drive, so I quickly made my way downstairs. He had showered, smelling of inexpensive aftershave, but I preferred it to that of his Father's. We sat back in the garden under the tree, very few words uttered between us until the first star appeared.

Tipping my head back I focused on the bright light above me. "It will be early in the morning in Australia."

"Have you heard from him?"

I shook my head, "Maybe tomorrow."

"I was convinced this tree had died, Matty."

"I knew it hadn't," I replied.

Silence returned, one by one the brothers and sisters of the first star came out to crowd the sky in a mass of pure brilliance.

"If you could wish, what would you wish for?"

He looked surprised when I answered, "I have my wish." I could feel him slightly recoil away from me, "I don't mean what's happened today."

He moved back closer again, taking a sigh of relief that the death of my Grandmother was not what I meant. My eyes began to feel heavy, tiredness and exhaustion was now hitting me.

"I need to get some sleep. I'll show you to your room."

He followed me inside, collecting his overnight bag from the hallway. I took him to his room. He did not flinch at the owl staring out towards the unlocked door. The smell of lavender still lay heavy in the room.

"A bit more fragrant than foxes," he laughed out loud.

I left him to settle in, thinking that Lizzie may still be up I went downstairs and called her.

"Hi Matty, I thought you'd disappeared off the face of the earth." She sounded sulky and not her normal vibrant self.

"Signal round here is rubbish, but I've got something to tell..."

I never had chance to finish my sentence, she launched into a tirade about how the spotty boy was a cheat and she never wanted to see him again. I listened, not daring to interrupt as profanities came down the line, words that seemed ugly coming from such a pretty mouth.

"And you'll never guess what, Matty?"

"What?" I was allowed that word at least.

"He's got a girl pregnant!"

She continued with no time for me to say "I told you so."

"Well I've got my own back, I'm dating her brother." I feared her cackling would wake Peter.

"Oh..."

"Is that all you can say, oh? Well, Matty, he's much better looking than that pizza faced idiot I was seeing before. He's got the most gorgeous Great Dane, obviously you wouldn't like it, your chest would go into overdrive."

"Perhaps he's the one for you then."

"I must admit, he's rather cute."

"Hmmm, him or the dog?"

"Ha ha ha, you are funny, so what's the news from Wales. Has the old witch behaved herself?"

"Dad's coming back. I'll be home in the next two or three days."

There was no way I could tell her, the connection between us had somehow been lost. She'd waved me off as her friend who lacked feeling, never showing interest in life or love: I now stood in the hallway feeling like a grown woman, passionate to survive and to learn more about life. How could I explain this to her, or anyone else who knew me before?

"Anyway Lizzie, just thought you should know."

"Ooh fab, you can tell me all about it when you get back. I best shoot, I'm expecting a call from him any minute."

"See you soon."

Click... The receiver went down.

I made sure the kitchen door was left open before I went up to my room, no longer afraid of howls in the night or ghosts that didn't exist. It wasn't long before I heard the sound of paws coming up the stairway. Peter's snoring comforted me, I was safe in the knowledge he was in a deep sleep and the soft pit pat would not waken him. Midnight lay at the foot of my bed, his coat dusty from digging and foraging for food. The pungency of fox filled the room, sour and heavy I breathed it in. My lungs expanded, opening wide to take in more of his earthy perfume. My chest rose and fell steadily, soon my eyes closed, and I listened to the rhythm of his breathing; we were in unison with sleep coming to us both.

CHAPTER 26

Wake up child from solemn sleep
Embrace the day from all who weep
A mother's womb can soon betray
And bare once more your bleakest day.

I'd packed by the time Peter woke. Midnight left before dawn, he had whispered in the night that a meeting would be held and I was to attend. I was to listen out for his call before I went to Laugharne. Reaching out for his fur, the morning birds chorus told me he'd departed, my hands fell only on the quilt that was my Mother's. This tuneful alarm broke all menace of flying nightmares. I revelled in the beauty of their song and not their torment. It was a glorious day, the sun's heat was kept from being unbearable by a cool breeze. Light filtered through every window I opened, the lavender rooms awoke from their deathly sleep. The house, like myself, was wakening to a new day. Hope, laughter and happiness may finally enter through its front door. I would bring my Mother back here, showing her how beautiful the house could be, with a lick of paint it could be a second home. Tonight I would be reunited with her, passing on sad news, but showing her the change in me. If she'd heard about my Grandmother's death then she would surely have called me.

There was still no news from my Father, perhaps the police had made contact and he was already on a plane bound for home. I found Peter in the back room, staring vacantly at the covered mirror.

"Did you sleep ok?" I asked.

He never turned to answer, "Ok, thanks. I don't remember this being covered up when Dad was here?"

"I want you to take it away and burn it, along with all the stuffed birds that are in the guest rooms."

He eventually turned towards me, his eyes bleary and bloodshot, "I quite like the owl."

"Then keep it. I'm sure it will remind you of Gwyneth."

There was a long silence, maybe he was weighing up if my sarcasm would continue.

"What time do you want to go to Laugharne?"

"You can drop me off about seven."

"What do you mean drop you off? I thought I was staying, I thought you may want to see Dylan's place, it'll be shut by then."

I swallowed hard, this was going to be more difficult than I realised, "I need to be on my own, Peter."

He gave me a look of anger, I felt unnerved and stepped back, "I feel responsible for you, Matty, until your Dad gets back. For God's sake you can't travel back on your own."

"Well I'll ask Sara if she will give me a lift, if that makes you feel better."

He stepped towards me, his bloodshot eyes fuelled more by rage. "So it's ok for her to be with you and not me, and what the bloody hell do you want to go there for?"

The distant high pitch scream stopped him in his tracks, he stared out towards the garden.

"I have to go out for a bit, Peter."

"I know where you're going, Matty, back to see those bloody foxes. Whoever fired that gunshot before could do it again, and next time it could be you with a bullet hole through your chest."

I evaded his stare. "Get some rest, I won't be out long."

I expected him to stop me leaving, his face so tight with anger, but his eyes returned to the window.

"Do as you wish," he muttered.

As I walked down the drive towards the road I glanced over my shoulder, my heart began to race as I quickly gained speed. I took one final look behind me, before I crossed over towards the gate, to check I wasn't being followed. If I was to die in this field I wished for a clean instant kill, not a lingering death in hospital where Mother would weep for the conversations we would have no more. The flowers had been crushed by yesterday's downpour, my feet trod on stems too battered to care. I halted when I reached the green circle, far more foxes had gathered than before, and each one had its eyes on me. Midnight stood in the middle, tall and proud, a king amongst the others. I made my way towards him, the others nervously stepping back.

A voice barked inside my head, it came from one I had not seen before. He had more white than the others, his face pointed and sharp, there was hostility in his eyes.

"Tell her. Tell her now!"

Midnight bared his teeth and snapped towards the fox. *"Silence. Know your place."*

The angry beast recoiled and cowered back into the crowd with the others, I could sense there was something wrong, they were not just nervous or fearing another gunshot, something was troubling them and they looked towards Midnight for reassurance.

"We have to leave, this place is no longer safe for any of us." His distinctive tone echoed through my head.

"You can't leave, you said you would stay with me. Tonight I'll see my Mother and I will bring her back to you, then we can lead you to the safe place."

"The smell of death hangs in the air, too heavy for our kind. We must move on and find our own destiny without the fear of you humans hunting us anymore."

"You can't desert us, you CHOSE us both." Tears tumbled down my face, desperation forced me to my knees. I stretched my arms out to all of them. *"Free me from the solitude I was born with."*

Midnight stepped towards me, his rough tongue brushed against my cheeks licking away the salt water from a destroyed girl.

"I've fought with my Council, but they could not be persuaded. I was born to rule them and now they want me to lead them away. Perhaps you will find some of our kind when you return to your own homeland."

Forgetting to use my thoughts I screamed, "I have lost my Grandmother and now I am losing you!"

He hadn't understood my screams, controlling my tears I concentrated and directed my thoughts towards him. *"Tomorrow will be different, you will see."*

"At sun down we will be gone."

It was too late, his warm face withdrew from mine, returning to stand alongside his brothers and sisters. Despair like no other hit me, my ability to show love for these creatures was cruelly being taken away. Solitude was my destiny, I prayed for the gunman to put that bullet in my head. I ran and with each stride my arms pounded the air in front of me. Jumping the gate, I sped up the hill, my vision blurred by returning tears.

The grey gravel of the driveway scattered as I stumbled towards the front door. I tried to steady my hand to hold the key in the lock, but it was too late, Peter flung the door open. He gaped at me in horror as I ran past him up the stairs to my bedroom. I could hear him behind me, I made it up to my room just in time, slamming the door behind me before he had chance to enter.

"I told you not to go."

"Go away."

There was a knock at the door. "Please let me in, I need to know you're ok."

I breathed in deeply, trying to slow down my heartbeat before it burst out my chest.

"I'm… I'm…" Another deep breath, "I'm fine now."

"You don't look fine."

Rather than give him the satisfaction of being right I answered.

"Crows, the meadow was full of them. It reminded me of yesterday."

I could hear him shuffling behind the door, I feared at any minute the door handle would turn.

His voice softened, "Can I come in just to make sure you're alright?"

"Honest Peter, it was just seeing them again, it brought it all back to me." I prayed my voice sounded convincing, it was a feasible excuse. "I'm beginning to hate birds, full stop."

"Hmm and me." His soft warm lilt had returned, I took a sigh of relief.

"I'll be down later after I've had a shower, it must be gone lunchtime and we've not eaten."

"I'll go and see what's in and do us some lunch."

I heard him move slowly away from the door and descend down the stairs. A few minutes passed before I peered out. The sound of cupboards being opened downstairs meant he was now in the kitchen and I'd got away with another lie.

The shower water was scorching, I'd turned it up as high as it would go, masking my tear flushed face. By the time I'd put on my silk blouse and jeans all traces of blood had gone. I could blame looking slightly pink on the old plumbing and not being able to work the temperature control.

He'd laid the breakfast table with an assortment of grazing foods, cheese, pâté and bread had been neatly arranged amongst jars of pickles. Pretending to be hungry, I chewed furiously; holding down the queasiness I managed a half smile in-between mouthfuls.

"This is good, thank you."

"I'm no cook I'm afraid."

"It's too warm for a cooked meal," I said, dabbing my finger on the plate, picking up the last remaining crumbs. He studied me hard as I wiped my mouth on the back of my hand.

"I wonder what time it is?" He asked.

I showed him the screen on my phone "15:23 exactly."

In four hours and thirty-seven minutes I would be with her; my obsession for time was returning.

"Right, I'll go and burn that bloody mirror you hate so much."

The sun from the open kitchen door played across his face, his wide smile had returned and I'd fooled him. Leaving him to gather up wood from the garden shed, I returned to my bedroom. We'd both agreed that the bottom of the garden would be the ideal place for a fire, well away from the tree that was now overloaded with blossom.

The book that Sara had given me still lay on the dressing table, its three silver rings glistened from the incoming sun. My fingers caressed them, this holy book contained images of which I would never become. Sadness returned as I flicked to the last page, the image of the red haired child lovingly holding a fox brought back tears. I felt marooned and desolate, Midnight had turned his back on me and already I could feel my old self returning. Coldly, and not caring, I tore the page from the book, it crumpled in my hands, the parchment making a satisfying crunch between my fingers.

The smell of burning wood wafted through the window, taking away all scent of Midnight. My anger at being deserted carried me through the rest of the afternoon. I lay on the bed, my mind whirring with how I would explain to my Mother that the Trinity had turned its back on me. The *gift* that had briefly been given was now wrapped back up in a box, never to be opened again.

There was a knock at the door.

"Matty, it's 6:15 shall we head off soon?"

"I'll see you downstairs in a minute."

I waited until his footsteps became distant before changing, the silk blouse looked ridiculous and was quickly replaced by a plain T-shirt to match my face. He was already outside waiting for me, under one arm was the owl, both back doors of the van were wide open.

"Your taxi awaits, madam."

"I'm not getting in the back with all your garden rubbish."

He squawked, his arms outstretched with the bird of prey, "This is going in the back unless you want to carry it on your lap."

I hadn't got time for his humour, slamming the front door behind me, I made my way to the passenger door and got in. Peter was now clambering in the back, moving ladders and machinery to make way for his new best friend.

I heard the back doors shut. "All done!" he shouted.

He climbed into the driver's seat then put the key in the ignition, the engine shuddered then let out a roar before turning to a low rumble.

"Your van's a mess, I doubt you'll find the owl again." I said, peering into the rear-view mirror.

He leant over to me, his tongue stuck out like a spoilt child. "It will fly out," he retorted.

We slowly pulled off the drive and made our way down the hill, I glanced briefly over as we passed the gate. It would no doubt be my last sighting, soon I would be home along with my Mother. He drove in silence, I avoided any glances, my head leant against the partially open passenger window.

As we passed the caravan park he finally spoke. "Can you smell something?"

I looked at him, his nose wrinkled in disgust. "It's probably the formaldehyde from the bird," I said. I took a deep breath in, the smell of grass cuttings that I'd previously noticed was now overpowered by another. I sniffed at my bare arms, perhaps the shower gel had not been enough to take away Midnight's scent.

"You can smell it as well, eh?" He said tapping his fingers on the steering wheel.

I didn't respond straight away, I was overwhelmed by sadness. The smell of a fox was the only reminder I would ever have of compassion.

"Can't smell a thing," I replied.

We continued on, the hill down to Laugharne was before us. Peter changed gear as we descended into the town. Our silence was interrupted by a loud thudding sound from the back of the van. Ladders banged against each other, we both flinched in unison.

"What the hell was that?" I asked.

"Bloody owl's probably tried to take off," he grinned.

I looked over my shoulder to see upturned tins of paint, the ladders rested precariously on top of them.

"I would secure the ladders if I were you," I muttered.

"I'll wait until we stop."

We pulled into the car park, it was completely empty and I felt intoxicated with the panoramic view before me. Even though Peter had seen its beauty many times before, his mouth dropped in awe at the landscape he called home.

"Something's wrong," he said pointing out towards the distant water that was now turning. The inlets were waiting, soon the sea would fill them, raising the moored up boats ready to sail.

"What's wrong?" I asked bemused.

"No birds, not one."

My eyes scoured the horizon, then gradually I raised them upwards. It was true, the sky above billowed with grey clouds, but was bird-less; no sandpipers or herons swooped or dived. Not one seagull squawked or fought over the washed-up remnants of a dead crab.

"I've had enough of things that fly to last me a lifetime," I muttered under my breath.

"Perhaps a storm is due," he replied.

"I hope not, I haven't brought a coat."

The clock in the middle of the dashboard showed 6:45pm. In one hour and fifteen minutes I would be in her arms. My stomach churned nervously as I reflected on the last twelve months.

His eyes were curious, "You still haven't told me why you wanted to come here."

"I told you, I just need some time alone to think about all that's happened. Sara said she would bring me back later." My eyes bored into his, there was no way he could tell I was spinning a lie.

"Ok, I'll just get out and sort the ladders then leave you in peace," he smiled.

We climbed out, I soaked in the silence before me, as Peter made his way to the back of the van. The doors swung open followed by a loud clatter, "Damn it!" He shouted.

I walked round, curious to see what had caused him to curse. The owl had tumbled out onto the car park, one wing had been badly crushed under the weight of the ladders.

"Give it to Gwyneth, she'll know how to fix it. I'm sure she'll be pleased to see you," I said with a hint of sarcasm.

"No thanks, I'll sort it myself." Peter scowled, he picked up the bird then carefully wrapped it in a dust sheet before replacing it back in. He climbed into the van, fastening the ladders with rope, each one securely tied to the other.

"There, that should do it." He jumped back out closing the doors behind him, a bead of sweat trickled from his brow.

I studied his face; I would miss the freckles and the twinkle in his eye.

"I want to thank you, Peter."

"What for?"

"For taking care of me."

Brushing my cheek with his hand he smiled, "That's what friends do."

I almost smiled.

"See you soon," I said.

"I damn well think so. Make sure you get a lift back or call me."

I nodded then waited for him to get back in the driver's seat. The engine made its familiar roar as he turned the van around, he then gave a final wave, before disappearing from view.

CHAPTER 27

Laugharne was not only abandoned by birds, but also people. As I looked over to the town square I noticed the empty cobble streets. The bistro had a closed sign outside and the shutters were pulled down on the pub windows. A solitary ginger cat ambled across the road, confident that the busy traffic allowed him to take his time.

I made my way across the small bridge next to the castle. The water underneath it gently bubbled across large pebbles covered in green algae. I paused to look over, small minnows darted in-between the shadows. My phone told me it was 19:00, I'd hoped that the next hour would give me enough time to reach the old boathouse.

Water was already seeping in between the large boulders and salt grey shingle that started the incline towards Dylan's house. My trainers slipped across one large rock, it was already sucking in the life of the estuary, moistening the moss and lichens, and bringing them back to life. I could now see the largest mud plane, it was engulfed in water. Soon the tide would be in. I thought for a minute, realising that soon the path would be cut off and there would be no turning back. Confident in the knowledge my Mother would know another way to the town, I raised my head to the sun for one last time. The steep steps in front of me were carved deep into the rock face, a tall metal sign stood proud at their base, *Dylan's Boathouse this way*. I clung onto the winding rusty rail and hauled myself up the first step, my body burned with urgency to reach the top. Repeating to myself, "Just a few minutes more," I took the final step to the top of the cliff face. The hand rail was now gone, replaced by an old stone wall that ran steeply down to the water's edge. I passed an old green shed with another sign post, *The Writing Shed*. There wasn't time to peer through the cobwebbed windows, even though I was curious. Soon this small construction was a blur behind me, Dylan's boathouse loomed ahead. Jutting out across the estuary, its shingled tiled roof glistened from the reflecting water below. Around it ran a balustrade of timber, a resting place for visitors to gaze and long to be an aspiring poet. The metal gate to the entrance was padlocked, a chalkboard sign had been propped crudely against it *Closed until further notice*. I puzzled as to why it didn't give any explanation, visualising the disappointed looks on the weary trekkers faces, I moved on.

The path changed from stone to grass, the wall replaced by young trees, overgrown shrubbery and hedges. I headed into woodland, each step took me further into a dimmer light. Occasionally I saw a shimmer of yellow in-between the entangled canopy of leaves above me, it was soon gone, I was plunged from summer into autumn. Decaying leaves carpeted the way before me, starved of heat and light they crumpled with age. Honeysuckle poked through the brambles either side, its smell suffocated by the mouldy sodden ground.

Silence was now all around, the only sound was that of my breathing. The nape of my neck ran sticky with sweat as I carried on walking. It must be nearly eight o'clock and there was no sign of the Old Boathouse. I called out her name, pausing in the solitude of the woodland around me; there was no reply. In the distance I could see a clearing, to the right of it stood a tall metal crisscross barrier fence. It was becoming softer underfoot, my trainers tried to grip the sodden leaves as I pounded my way forward. As I approached the metal fence a distinctive smell hit me, my nostrils no longer filled with woodland compost, but a light perfume; it was my Mother's and she must be near. A large notice hung from one section of the fence.

This is private property, trespassers will be prosecuted.

I peered through the gaps of the barrier overgrown with thicket, I could just about make out the cliffside running down to the estuary. Two sections of the barrier had been moved, the grooves in the soil were fresh showing someone had recently forced them open. Excitement charged through me as I called out, "Mom it's me. I'm here!"

I thought I heard a noise behind me, I spun round and lost my footing in the mud. I fell backwards into the fence, my body hit the metal with a loud clatter, the echo announcing my arrival. I sat there on the squelching ground, waiting for whoever was following me to appear. I wasn't afraid, only ashamed that I'd allowed myself to get dirty. My Mother knew how much I detested the slightest mark on my clothes. That was the old Martha, well before I had lain in fields of foxes and inhaled the countryside, she would understand. She would love me more for it. Minutes passed before I hauled myself up, clinging onto the metal with both hands for stability. The force of my fall had parted the gap even more, enabling me to walk through, I was now on the other side.

Light was beginning to disappear around me, I fumbled for my phone. My empty pockets told me I must have dropped it when I fell. I would be late, she would wonder what had happened to her time obsessed child, yet another let down to explain.

In front of me was the beginning of small steps that had been crudely cut out of the rock-face, they spiralled downwards towards the estuary. I made my way down, the smell of her perfume became stronger with each step. I was halfway down when I saw it, the skeleton of an old boathouse stood below me. Set deep against the cliff its terracotta flooring formed a plateau out onto the estuary. Where once stood walls, lay ruins of broken bricks and rubble, barely outlining the boundaries of what would have been a magnificent boathouse. To the side of the house was a large lawn, a green playground for the residents who once lived there. Now it was home to a colony of rabbits, idly grazing on the long lush grass as they ignored my presence.

My mind drifted back to my Mother's diary, this must be the place she came to with Sara, exchanging presents on that cold winter's day. This was the special place she wanted to buy and renovate, this was where she now would be.

I clambered further down calling out, my words ringing across the estuary, water lapped against the pillars of the house. I heard her, beckoning me gently.

"I'm here, Matty. Come down."

Almost at once I spotted in the distance, her lilac frame flecked by the disappearing sun, she sat facing outwards gazing across the water. The terracotta tiles clashed against her dress, her knees tucked under her chin, red curls spiralled down her shoulders. Time had lengthened her hair, it was the one thing that matched the floor she was sitting on.

I thought for one minute my heart would stop, not giving me a chance to make the final steps. This was the beginning of the end, a mystery that had shadowed every day of my past year. Yearning for Midnight to be beside me, a generation of *Chosen*, I slowly made my way down.

She extended her arm out, her delicate pale wrist supported fine silver bangles. She was waving for me to approach, they jangled with each movement. The old tiles moved underneath me as I ran towards her, age had not been kind to them, I knew she would restore this old place back to its former glory.

I was two feet away, the lilac dress fell over her ankles covering her delicate feet. Soon she would turn, taking me in her arms so I may breathe in her motherhood.

"It's not like you to be late," she whispered.

I looked down in shame, my pulse raced through my temples.

"I lost my phone on the way here."

She gasped, "Not your lifeline, Matty?"

She threw her head back and let out a laugh, the shadow from the cliff-face obliterated her beautiful features. I felt a coldness run through me, not because the sky had become grey, there was something else chilling in the air.

"Mom, please tell me where you've been?" I pleaded.

"I've been here all the time," her voice cracked becoming deeper and coarse.

"You sound different, Mom."

Still with her back turned she sternly said, "And YOU, are YOU different, have you learned to laugh and cry yet?"

I understood what she meant, had her child become part of the Trinity. My voice was tentative and apologetic.

"Yes, I became different, they chose me Mom, but…"

"But what?"

"They have suffered so much, hunted and shot until they could bear no more. I've let you down, they've gone."

Silence fell between us for what seemed like an eternity, I held back the urging sobs that desperately wanted to flow. It was soon broken… *tap*… *tap*… *tap* went her fingers on the tiles, then screeched as she dragged her nails backwards and forwards. I took another step closer, now the perfume was strong and intoxicating.

"So you're alone? They didn't come with you?"

"Yes, I'm alone."

She let out a sigh, her chest heaved upwards and downwards slowly. "Good."

Moving her hands forward she pushed herself up to a standing position, something metallic clattered to the floor below her. With her back still towards me she bent down and picked it up. A year ago I would have towered above her, a giant of a child. Now her head was above mine, confused I stared at her feet to see what heels she was wearing. The long lilac dress made it impossible. I reached out touching her shoulder, it felt bony and under nourished, the coldness of her flesh made me recoil.

Her head twisted to one side letting out a growl that stopped me in my tracks. Slowly she turned, bit by bit I could see the beginnings of her face. The red curls now exposed a hair line of brown strands. The ivory skinned face that contorted towards me was Sara's, her mouth twisting with anger and rage. In her hands she held a rifle, the barrel now resting against my forehead.

"You stupid bitch," she hissed. "You should know better than to touch me."

I heard the click of the safety catch, her fingers poised to squeeze and end my life. My breastbone ached from my thundering heartbeat, if I moved she would no doubt pull the trigger.

Minutes passed as we stood frozen to the spot, her eyes flashed wildly, occasionally glancing over my shoulder to see if we were alone.

A single tear fell down my cheek, I couldn't move to brush it away. Realising that I would soon be dead, I mustered what I thought would be my final words.

"Why?"

She looked bemused and let out a howl. I closed my eyes realising this would be the last sound I would ever hear.

"Why not?"

The barrel moved slightly away from between my eyes, sliding across my forehead as if to caress it.

"Please, before you kill me, tell me where is my Mother?"

"Ah, your glorious Mother, the one who had everything, looks, the love of my fiancé and most of all the *Gift*. For years I longed to whisper in an animal's ear and hear it reply."

The roughness of the barrel scratched at my skin, exposing it to the air, which stung like a swarm of bees.

"I became a vet in the hope that someone would bring their beloved pet to me. I longed for them to tell me their symptoms or tell me stories of how their owners lived their lives. The fatal needle of death was easy if it chose not to speak." Her throat gurgled as she choked on regurgitating spit.

I swallowed the salt from my tears.

"I was born like you and your Mother, some may say *strange,* so when Meredith told me she'd been *Chosen* I realised I could be as well. It was only a matter of time."

I gathered up what little courage I had left, remembering how my Father had told me of a case he'd been working on where a man had caught a burglar in his house; the intruder was carrying a shotgun. After an hour's gentle discussion, the man had managed to persuade his perpetrator to put down his gun.

"So you still could be *Chosen*? That's why Mother loved you so much."

I heard her shuffle backwards, screeching and spitting phlegm to the floor. I cautiously opened my eyes, the gun was still poised towards my head. Her cold cruel eyes briefly changed, she tilted her head to one side anticipating me telling her more.

"She said that you were like a sister to her and if anything should happen to her you would look after me." My lies over the past few days had put me in good stead, I almost convinced myself I was telling the truth.

The gun lowered. Sara paced backwards and forwards, cursing to herself that she shouldn't listen. I realised the bracelets she wore, that crashed against the rifle, belonged to my Grandmother.

The back of my T-shirt dripped with sweat as I waited for her to answer. She paused before raising the gun again.

"Ha, Meredith told me the same, just before I blew her brains out."

With those words I knew my life had ended, even if she somehow became struck with a moment of compassion and spared me, I could not go on, Mother was never coming back.

Something behind us startled her, wildly she raised the rifle above my head, footsteps were approaching.

"Put the gun down, Sara."

I had nothing to lose, so I turned to see who was speaking. Michael stood a few feet away from us, by his side was PC Matthews.

"Oh good, a party," she whispered towards me.

Michael reached out his hands begging for her to listen. "You've got this all wrong, Sara. Let me explain."

"Ha, explain. For years I've had to listen to your mutterings, talking in your sleep about the beautiful woman with red hair who was supposed to be my friend. How much you longed to see her, and how I wouldn't understand. I found the letter you'd drafted telling her the boathouse could be hers. The stupid cow believed me hook, line and sinker when I wrote and told her I was you and would sell it. Even when I offered to pick her up from the station and bring her here to meet you, she babbled with excitement. All she cared about was making this a place for herself and those bloody foxes."

My stomach coiled, Michael hadn't shot Midnight's vixen, she had. My eyes pleaded into his for forgiveness, if I was to die he needed to know I was sorry. His eyes were not on me, but on her.

"She was my sister, how could I not love her."

For one moment I thought she would drop the gun, she stumbled backwards, her mouth wide open in disbelief, my eyes mirrored hers.

"I was born before her, our Mother was barely fifteen when she became pregnant, she gave me away out of shame. She then met Meredith's father and married, the rest is history. I was a teenager when my adopted Mother told me who my real Mother was and that she lived in Pendine. Meredith didn't know, for years I watched her growing up, longing to tell her, but now she'll never know."

What the hell was he talking about? I stared hard into his green eyes, the same colour as the woman who had sung lullabies to me at bed-time. The same eyes that sparkled on Sunday afternoons, as she sat next to my Father. If he was my uncle, then this made Peter my cousin. I felt sick at the thought of my lips on his.

Matthews spoke calmly, not once flinching at the waving gun.

"A police boat will be here any minute, if you hand yourself in now then maybe there's a chance we can get you some treatment. The judge may look more kindly on you if you're willing to get help."

How did they know I would be here? My mind whizzed with endless possibilities, none made any sense.

I could hear her steps coming towards me again, the silver on her wrists giving her away, her sour breath fell against the nape of my neck. She hissed into my ear, "I gave that crazy witch of a Grandmother a chance to tell you to go. She sure was a fighter… ha ha ha."

The barrel was pushed into the back of my head, Michael and Matthews stared in horror as she poised herself to pull the trigger. I closed my eyes and prayed for death to come quickly.

CHAPTER 28

I never heard him arrive; only the smell of soil and protection alerted me to his presence. At first I thought she'd fallen, snapping the bones of her legs against the terracotta tiles. His screams overpowered hers; razor sharp teeth sank deep into the flesh of her ankles. His burnt red coat matched the floor she wriggled on, wildly he savaged her body, relentlessly tugging at her flesh. He shook his head violently from side to side; fragments of lilac cotton flew into the air. I read his mind as he took each bite; he wanted revenge for the death of his kind and my Mother. I watched Midnight's power as he pulled at her blood stained lilac dress, dragging her, her arms flailing in a futile attempt to strike at him. Small pools of blood gathered with each movement as he pulled her nearer to the edge of the boathouse. Matthews and Michael stared open-mouthed in disbelief as she cried out for help. I smiled, oddly transfixed by what I was witnessing. I could have stopped him, but I didn't. Matthews leapt forward to grab the rifle, his hands shook as he aimed the barrel at his target. I realised his intent was not to kill Sara, but my one true friend. I launched myself forward, making a wall between him and the barrel.

"Get out of the way!" Matthews bellowed.

I stood rigid, I could hear Sara squirming behind me. The growls of Midnight overshadowing the sound of the estuary water lapping against the house. I turned, giving him permission with my thoughts to finish what he'd started. He took one final lunge at her. In desperation she writhed backwards, her legs now submerged in the water. She grabbed frantically at the marsh grass, twisting her fingers around the coarse blades, she clung on with pale bloody hands. Midnight sank his teeth into the knuckles of her hand, she gasped in pain, begging me to help her. The water now surrounded her neck, her legs attempted a kicking movement, desperate to keep her afloat, but soon they became submerged as the muddy water dragged them down. Her eyes rolled backwards, showing only a blank white stare.

Then suddenly, her face changed from terror to complete madness.

"Voices!" she called. "I can hear a thousand voices!"

Water spewed from her mouth as she gasped for air, her head dipped into the water then rose again. We watched as she let go of the marsh grass, the tide sending her further away from us.

"They are calling me." Water was now in her throat, her words gurgled.

A dark wave rose above her head, engulfing her in one swoop, the tips of her fingers slowly faded down into the inky black water below. Small bubbles appeared and then she was gone. I felt no remorse.

Midnight edged back from the water, his eyes still fixed outwards making sure she wasn't going to reappear. Michael was now by my side, gripping my hand tightly in his. The skin of man who I had cruelly accused of being a killer now felt warm. He was my Mother's brother and she never knew; he wanted her to have this place she truly loved. My tears flowed like the estuary, as I thought back to the photograph I'd found of my Grandmother holding a baby. He was now the grown man stood next to me. We had both been robbed by jealousy. I pushed my fingers deep into the palm of his hand, telling him I was sorry.

Matthews stood behind us, the rifle still primed to fire at Midnight.

Midnight began sniffing the ground where the terracotta tiles lay. He stopped a foot away from Matthews who aimed the barrel at his head.

"Stop!" I screamed. "There has been enough blood spilt." My eyes pleaded with his, he glanced towards Michael.

"Put it down, Matthews!" he shouted.

I let out a sigh of relief as the rifle dropped from his shaking hands. Unfazed Midnight continued to sniff the ground, his paws began frantically scratching away at the broken tiles. Every few seconds he would stop and take another sniff. He let out a howl as his mouth grasped something shiny that lay buried a few inches down. We watched as he lifted his muddied snout up, a broken silver chain dangled from his mouth. I let go of Michael's hand and raced over to him, opening my palm for his blood stained mouth to drop the object in. At the end of the chain was a silver fox.

"This is my Mother's, she must be here," I said, my eyes blurred with tears. In the distance I could hear the sound of a boat engine bumping across the water, it was approaching fast.

"We've been following Sara for a while, Martha. Michael came forward a few weeks after your Mother went missing. He alerted us of her strange behaviour, she was threatening to blackmail him and frame him for your Mother's disappearance, but we had no proof. Bringing you here seemed to be the only way to draw her out."

Michael put his arm round my shoulder, "I'm so sorry, it was the only way."

Confused and full of rage I stumbled backwards, I'd been used as bait to be hunted like a fox.

By now the light had completely faded, floodlights from the approaching boat lit up the frame of the old boathouse. I could just about make out the words POLICE on its port. I wasn't going to leave before I had more answers.

"But you took my phone away. You had a chance to catch her then."

Matthews nodded, "We were able to trace the call, but we needed you to believe differently, that's why we deleted all evidence of it."

"I don't understand." Tears of frustration streamed down my cheeks.

"Your Father told us you were unable to lie, if Sara had asked you if we were investigating, you would have said yes. By removing all trace of the call you lost faith in us, maybe even questioning if you ever received it and only trusting yourself."

"You acted on your own, Matty, but we've been by your side all the way," Michael whispered gently.

The words *your Father*, pierced me like a knife. He knew all along and was part of the hunt. My eyes quickly searched around the old ruin for Midnight, I longed to hold something I trusted, but he was gone.

The boat finally came to a halt as it anchored itself alongside the boathouse, at its stern stood four uniformed officers. Behind them was a tall grey haired man holding a blanket, I recognised the chiseled features, they belonged to my Father.

Michael and Matthews strode towards the boat expecting me to follow. I stayed firmly on the spot watching as my Father waved. He was expecting me to go running into his arms. Matthews looked back and called to me "Let's get you home, Martha."

Remembering a film I had once watched as a child, I closed my eyes and whispered *"There's no place like home."* I slowly opened them, the silhouettes of broken walls and rubble were all around me, my feet felt the warmth of the once magnificent floor. In the distant corner I saw a small shape, moving in and out of the shadows. Without hesitation, I ran towards it, my hands reaching out to hold what I hoped would be him. As I got nearer, a small and delicate shape stepped out of the darkness. The young vixen pressed her head against my hand, her eyes resembled two emeralds set deep into a band of gold.

I heard her words.

"You are home, Martha."